Shock held Cleo
rooted to the spot

Luc! After all these years! She had taken a new job, come to a new country, left all the agony of loss and betrayal behind her. And yet, by some twist of chance, she had met Luc again.

Her eyes met and locked with his. His glance was cold and indifferently appraising. There was a drumming in her ears and the great thump of her heart was a physical pain. As she took the proffered chair gratefully, there was a moment when he could have acknowledged her as his wife.

But the moment passed, as Cleo knew it would.

Luc did not intend to know her, which meant that she dared not know him....

OTHER
Harlequin Romances
by JANE ARBOR

Late Rapture

by

JANE ARBOR

Harlequin Books

TORONTO • LONDON • NEW YORK • AMSTERDAM
SYDNEY • HAMBURG • PARIS

Original hardcover edition published in 1978
by Mills & Boon Limited

ISBN 0-373-02251-4

Harlequin edition published April 1979

CHAPTER ONE

EVERYTHING about the noon flight from London to Corsica had gone smoothly.

The giant jet had landed on schedule at Ajaccio; the passengers in transit had gone through Customs and Immigration there, and the little eight-seater plane which cut to minutes the several road-hours of distance to Bonifacio had been ready to be fussily away with its load of on-goers.

It was a clear April day. From the air the land-mass of Sardinia across the Strait was in full view, as was the southern coastline of Corsica, with its edging ribbon of yellow sands and its jagged chalk cliffs where Bonifacio's ancient citadel towered above quays and harbour dotted with colour and craft at anchor.

Some way east of the town the plane circled for its descent towards the single runway of an airport cut from as miniature a mould as itself. It came to a halt almost within touch of an office labelled *Aeroport Siccone* in big lettering, and the passengers stepped out on to sun-baked grass.

They nodded farewells to each other and waited in the open to collect their luggage from the hold of the aircraft. Waiting for her own, Cleo felt a touch on her shoulder and turned to be greeted by a pleasant-faced woman she judged to be in her early forties, who said with a smile, 'By elimination I take it you are Miss Tyndall? Right?'

Smiling back and offering her hand, 'Right,' Cleo confirmed. 'And you are——?'

'Anne Marlowe. Is that your bag coming out now? And you'll have been through all the official fuss at Ajaccio? Good. I've got the car outside. La Réserve is about twenty minutes' drive.'

As she straightened from stowing Cleo's luggage in the boot of the open car which stood on the approach tarmac Anne Marlowe threw the girl an appraising glance.

'At least the photograph you sent us didn't lie,' she said. 'You're quite the looker I'd hoped to find you. For in your job a bit of natural charm takes you a long way with people. That—and of course all the other skills our advertisement in *The Times* asked for!'

Cleo flushed at the praise of her appearance. 'Certainly you made the advertisement pretty detailed,' she agreed. 'And I think it was the opening, "Girl Friday Wanted", which really intrigued me.'

Her companion beamed. 'Yes, a stroke of genius, that. The Big Man's idea—our Director.'

'Your Director?'

'Oh, didn't you realise? Richard and I don't own La Réserve, you know. We're only managers. We live permanently in our villa on the estate. The Director comes and goes. But the development, the whole project of a holiday resort of villas and studios for rental, and a marina for yachtsmen, belongs to him; financed and organised by him from scratch. A go-getter, if ever there was one! But no, Richard and I came in by the same route as you have. We answered an advertisement for managing a holiday development on the south Corsican coast. That was three or four years ago, but the thing has mushroomed rewardingly since. Tell you all about ourselves one day. No time now. We've arrived.'

Anne broke off her staccato recital to wave a hand towards a wide gateway on the right of the road. She swept the car through on to a drive from which lesser paths branched and curved and mounted the steepening terrain, as did the drive itself between palms and eucalyptus and the gnarled boles of cork.

Here and there between the trees Cleo glimpsed little houses, each on its plateau of level ground, none of them cheek-by-jowl with their nearest neighbours.

'They're all built in the regional style of local wood.' Anne stabbed a finger towards two larger buildings. 'The Bureau, the Clubhouse—there . . .

and there. And here's your own place—just a one-roomed studio, but with all the doings and handy for everything. I'll see you in and show you how your gadgets work. You can do for yourself or eat in the restaurant; it backs on to the Clubhouse. But tonight Richard and I would like you to be our guest in the restaurant. Take your time now, and then perhaps you'll walk over to the office to meet Richard?'

Left to herself ten minutes later, Cleo prowled round the little domain which was to be her home for the next six months. It was of doll's house proportions—a daybed in the living-room, a tiny shower room, a narrow kitchen, hanging and store-cupboards, and a south-facing balcony opening off the living-room.

'All this and heaven too'—sun and sea and a job which should stretch her, in an idyllic place. As she unpacked and showered and changed she was conning over her commitments.

She had to be prepared to work every week-end, for that was when the villas' occupancy changed hands, and people had to be met at the airport, inventories to be checked and the cleaning of the villas supervised. She might be asked to take parties of youngsters swimming, or to baby-sit to give their parents a break. She must partner the partnerless, play errand-girl to the Marlowes, information-desk to the guests and to speak English or French according to need.

She thought back. It was a long time since she had used French equally with English. A long time. Nearly five years—An involuntary jerk of her head shook off a memory that could still hurt. Dutch, yes. A smattering of German—both from her experience as purser's assistant on the North Sea shipping run between England and Holland during most of those five years. But French? She would have to begin to think in that again now.

She walked down to the office in the early evening sunshine, aware all the way of the sweet, pervading scent on the air—from the myrtle and thyme and bay and rosemary, the *maquis* which was a delight in itself and whose name had gone into history.

She crossed the verandah of the office building, knocked at an inner door and obeyed the summons from inside.

A man who had been sitting at a desk drawn up to a french window rose and turned to greet her. A second man who had been facing him, leaning against the jamb of the window, arms folded, merely straightened slowly and looked across at her.

Her eyes met and locked with his, cold and indifferently appraising. There was a drumming in her ears and the great thump of her heart was a physical pain. From the edge of near-stupor she heard the first man introducing himself, 'I'm Richard Marlowe,' and then his companion, 'Luc

Vidame, our Director. Welcome to La Réserve, Miss Tyndall. Come and sit down.'

Luc! After all these years! A new job, a new country, all that agony of betrayal and loss behind her, and yet—Luc here by some twist of chance; Luc, totally unmoved at sight of her, more stony of face than any stranger, though he could not but recognise her, as she knew and yearned towards him. As she took the proffered chair gratefully, there was a moment when he could have acknowledged her. But the moment passed, as she knew it would. He did not intend to know her, which meant that she dared not know him.

Richard Marlowe sat down again, muttering, 'Some paperwork I have to do on you for the authorities, Miss Tyndall,' and drew some documents towards him, among them, face upwards, Cleo's own photograph in colour, as good a likeness as possible of the girl it portrayed.

Hair nearer to silver than true blonde, youthfully club-cut with a thick fringe curving above level brows; grey eyes surprisingly darkly lashed; high cheekbones just touched with colour shadowing the narrowing to jawline and chin. The boat-shaped neck of the dress she had worn left the spread of her shoulders partly bare; the cling of the material emphasised the swell of young breasts. The photograph cut off above her slim waist and the long slender line of her thighs.

Looking at it, Cleo realised that Luc had moved over to look at it too, standing above her. She looked deliberately at Richard Marlowe, prepared to give him the information he wanted. But it was Luc who began to question her, at first with conventional queries—Did she know Corsica at all? Had her flight out been good? From which English airport had she left?—all courtesies to a newcomer, but studied insolences addressed to her, who had lain in his arms, known his tenderness and passion, laughed with him, trusted him . . . been his wife.

His questions became more pointed, more searching.

'You'll have realised that when we advertised for a Girl Friday, we weren't going to be satisfied with anyone who hadn't all-round qualifications for the job?' he said.

She managed to look him straight in the eye. 'I think so. They were several and rather varied, but I thought I could fulfil most of them, so I applied for the post.'

'Most of them? Not all?' he pounced.

She acquiesced with a lowering of her lids. 'Very well, all—if you insist.'

' "All" happens to be important,' he snapped. 'It was also important that you understood why we asked of you all that we did. For instance, why you need a valid driving licence——'

At that point Richard Marlowe put in a word.

'I think you can take it, Luc, that we explained to Miss Tyndall that she might have to ferry people to and fro; that she needed to swim well, to take duty at the pool or at the shore. In her previous job she had had secretarial experience and in dealing with people, and as she was astute enough to answer the advertisement in English *and* good French, and she filled the age and pleasant looks bit, Anne and I agreed that she understood very well what we were looking for, and so we engaged her.'

'And the other stipulation—mine?' Luc asked smoothly.

His colleague looked slightly embarrassed. 'Yes, well—we included it, but we didn't enlarge on it.'

'Not considering it important that you shouldn't load yourselves with some star-crossed female using the job as an escape route from a steamy love-affair gone wrong?' Luc turned to Cleo. 'You were, I suppose, able to answer truthfully that at the time of applying you had no emotional entanglements, past, present or pending?'

She drew a long breath. 'I was,' she said. 'Entirely able.'

For a long moment his eyes held contact with hers. 'One hopes so,' he said.

He left before Richard Marlowe had finished his own questions to her. As he went out Richard asked, 'Will you dine with us, Luc? Miss Tyndall is joining us in the restaurant tonight.'

Luc declined, to Cleo's relief. Socially, across a dinner-table, she could *not* face him, and he had no right to be able to face her while he allowed her dilemma to continue. For he must be wholly responsible for it. At the first mention of her name by the Marlowes, a word from him could have prevented her being considered for the job. But he hadn't said that word. Why not? Because, aided by coincidence, he must have savoured the thought of confounding her with their meeting. *She* would be shocked by it; he would not. It would inevitably lead to her abandonment of an attractive job; was as subtle a revenge as he could have thought up, and in face of his silence, how could she not believe he had planned it so?

When she left the office she did not return to her own place, but took one of the many paths leading through the maquis, up to and beyond the last villa.

The path petered out where a little stream tumbled out from the scrub over a near-dry stony bed. She found a flat warm rock and sat on it, hands clasped round her knees. She had to think . . .

She couldn't stay, of course. She would have to concoct some tale of compelling urgency for her needing to leave to tell the Marlowes.

They would think her mad, inconsiderate, worse, but—— *Oh, Luc, Luc, why had you to*

*make it happen? Why had you to cheat me so?
What harm had I ever done you, except to marry
you for love; marry you, believing you loved me,
when all I was to you was use for a purpose—
your own purpose which I found out?*

The thought was a poignant cry from her
heart; the memory of their parting as clear as yesterday. But their meeting had come first—the unlikely meeting of a starry-eyed, young-for-her-age
eighteen-year-old girl with an elegant French
Riviera habitué whose invisible means of support,
whatever they were, were adequate enough to
keep him circulating in the jet-set throughout the
season.

Since she was sixteen, after her widowed
mother's death, Cleo had been the protegée of
her aunt, the much younger half-sister of Cleo's
father, by their father's second marriage. Olive
Tyndall had modelled as a career, had married a
rich Parisian, Roger Ravier, at twenty-five; had lost
him, and was in her widowed thirties when she
took Cleo into her luxurious Menton villa, and
found the addition to her household very useful
indeed.

Olive Ravier maintained a 'circle' of which she
was the lodestar but which entailed every con-
ceivable petty chore from her young niece.

Cleo paid bills or warded off creditors; checked
linen, stationery and flowers for guest-rooms,
ordered wine, wrote menus and invitations,

walked miniature poodles, ran daily errands for Olive, and regularly ate 'supper' in a breakfast-room instead of dinner with Olive's guests and was only co-opted to join a party when one of Olive's invitees had annoyingly let her down.

But that was what had happened on the night —probably one of many previous nights—when Luc had been there, and Cleo's place at table had been next to his.

He hadn't changed. He was as darkly handsome now as then. Sitting beside him that night she had been able to admire the swift flash of his full lids, his smile, his aquiline profile and the audacious jut of his chin as he talked to other people across the table. Then, kind, indulgent, he had talked to her, drawn her out, made her laugh. *Noticed her*. There had been a magic moment when, from the silver dishes of petits fours being passed round with the coffee, she had picked a fat marron glacé, had peeled off its foil and bitten into its sweetness.

Luc had been watching her. 'Do that again,' he had said.

'Do what?'

'Bite. Like that—with all your pretty front teeth at work.'

She had giggled, 'They're my absolute favourite sweetmeat,' and had done as she was told. Whereat he had made a long arm to the dish, pur-loined three more and dropped them with a con-

spiratorial wink into her lap. From that moment
she had loved him. He had been all her sun's rising, and somehow, unlikely as it should have
been that he should later even remember her
name, it had all seemed right that almost everywhere she went after that, he should be there.

She would be shopping in the market for
flowers and fruit, and he would be at the next
stall. She would be walking the poodles in the
Festival Gardens, and he would stroll in at the
gate. He treated her to ices on the Front, walked
her out to the old harbour and up into the foot-
hills behind the town. He had told her—which
she knew—that she was nothing but a Cinderella
to Olive, and that, by saving Olive the cost of a
social secretary, she had more than paid for her
keep.

And then, one never-to-be-forgotten day, he had
told her she was going to marry him, and the
miracle of his wanting her had been complete.

Olive had been furious, had called Cleo 'a little
fool' for deluding herself that a man of thirty or
so could possibly have fallen in love with her. Re-
putedly he was of good family, and seemed to
have enough money to keep himself. But a wife?
Had Cleo gone into that or about his future
plans? Cleo hadn't. All Luc had confided to her
was that the Riviera wasn't really his 'scene', and,
awake herself to its artificiality, she had been glad
about that. But for the rest she was content to

love and be loved—by Luc. And after she had
moved her few possessions from Olive's house,
she had never been invited to, nor entered it
again.

She had been married, French fashion, both in
church and by civil law, and had moved into
Luc's rented apartment in a block. On her wedding night she had been frightened and shy and
had even cried a little. But Luc had been all
understanding, all gentleness. His patient experience she had accepted without jealousy or ques-
tioning of it, since it had taught him how to rouse
her at last to a fierce response to the ardour with
which he wooed her . . . and took her in exquisite
surrender.

They had been golden honeymoon days, of
swimming and sailing and dawning companionship. Luc's English, practised in the English and
American set he mixed with, was more fluent
than was Cleo's French, but they used both. 'English is for everyday, French is for love,' Luc had
claimed, and had made it a sweet language for
wooing her.

A week or two after their marriage he had had
a birthday, his thirty-second. Cleo had scoured
the antique shops for a present and had chosen
a paperweight—a crystal swan on a mother-o'-
pearl 'lake', which Luc had declared was something he had always wanted, and of which he

made ostentatious use to clamp down his few personal papers.

A week after his birthday he had gone to Paris without her having made a teasing secret of his business there, but telling her that when he came back they would be leaving the Riviera for their 'real' life.

'I'm entitled to suspect you of going to visit another girl,' she had teased him.

He pulled a grotesque face. 'Not *one* girl. My harem of Oriental beauties.'

'Oh! How many do you keep in it?'

'At the last count——' He had broken off to lunge for her. 'Come here, you doubting little cabbage, and be kissed for just as many occupants as there were!'

So much for the miracle, the last of the dream. On the afternoon he was due back she had gone shopping for a special dinner menu to give him, and on the way back had stopped at a pavement café for an ice. On the table someone had discarded a copy of a notorious scandal-sheet, and she found herself idly regarding a paragraph in its gossip column. Each paragraph began coyly, 'We hear'—and this one continued,

'That there is no secret about the double coup recently brought off by the personable Luc Vidame of our seasonal set. It being imperative that, in order to inherit from a wealthy godparent, he should marry before his thirty-second birthday, it seems that, with little enough time to spare, he has done just that. Fortunately, in his hurried plunging of his hand into the lucky bean-bag of his feminine acquaintances, he has plucked out a charming if unknown *ingénue*. A double coup indeed, since the lady appears young enough to be biddable and modest in her demands—an importance, surely, to a young man of allegedly considerable extravagance? If no asset to his social life, she should not prove too great a burden . . .'

Cleo had blanched, re-reading the calumny over and over, mouthing the phrases half-aloud, trying to believe that her French was not equal to their meaning. But she knew it was. After two years in France she was bi-lingual to that extent. For instance, the description of Luc as *un cadet d'un haut appétit* meant just what she thought it did and implied—he needed money and a lot of it, and the rest followed. He had married her solely for the purpose of getting it. It was as simple as that.

Her first thought had been a passionate *No!* Her next, that she must confront Luc. If it weren't true, it should be actionable. If it were——! But she mustn't let herself even think it could be. She snatched up the journal and hurried home, wondering how she was going to endure the two hours before Luc could arrive from the airport.

She let herself into the vestibule of the apartment. Luc's valise stood on a chair there. He must have caught an earlier plane, for, through the open door of the salon, she could hear him talking in French to someone on the telephone, and in her new cruel suspicion of him, she listened.

He was agreeing, echoing something his correspondent had said.

'Congratulations in order? But of course! Dead easy, when it came to the point. Making a willing gift of herself, *la pauvre petite*. Utterly engaging ... disarming, that one should be so—What did you say? *Comme un fruit mûr?* Well, no, not quite like a ripe plum. More like a rather insecure green apple, so very immature, but so gratifyingly willing to fall, my young English bride of the trusting eyes.'

He had paused then. Cleo had waited, making no sound nor move, as he went on, 'And so, *mignonne*, there need be nothing now between you and Paris. I plan to move from here within a few days and we may be there before you. Yes ... Yes, I see. Very well, I'll ring you there. Wait for me to get in touch, and very soon, I promise you, I shall have done all I told you I would, and the rest will be up to you. Meanwhile—*bon voyage*.'

He had replaced the receiver and turning, saw Cleo. 'My cabbage,' he said, his arms wide to her. She came on unsmiling and handed him the paper, folded back to the gossip column. 'How true is that?' she demanded curtly.

Frowning, he glanced at the paper, then up at her. 'I didn't know you subscribed to the gutter press,' he said.

'I don't. I came by that by chance. But read it —*is it true?*'

He had read, then looked at her again. 'Substantially, yes,' he said.

Her heart plunged, her hope gone. But she still needed it spelled out. 'That you needed money; that, in order to get this inheritance, you had to marry before you were thirty-two? Is that so?'

'Yes.'

'And so you married me—only just in time?'

'Yes.'

With every monosyllable he uttered she had felt him withdrawing from her, closing his ranks against her. But she was past any appeal to him, any pleading to him to soften the truth.

'Without its mattering too much whether I was one girl or another? At that late date, *any* single one would have done?'

She had watched his lip curl cruelly. 'Within reason, perhaps. Though naturally a complete gargoyle might have proved a social embarrassment, mightn't she?' he sneered.

'Would it have mattered, since she was only a key to the money you couldn't get otherwise?' Cleo retorted as cruelly.

'I chose you, and you weren't unwilling,' he reminded her.

'No—because I'd fallen in love with you—or with the man I thought you were until I read—that,' she had flicked a finger at the paper, 'and until I heard you describe me to the girl-friend you're planning to meet in Paris as an immature green apple, only too ready to fall into your lap —or should it be your *trap*?'

She had meant to startle him and obviously she had. He glanced back at the telephone. 'You were listening in just now?'

'And heard you call her "darling".'

'*Mignonne*, yes. That is——'

'I don't want to know,' she cut him short.

'And I've no intention of telling you *anything* in order to placate you in this mood,' he declared, his tone so savage that she almost quailed. But she rallied her pride.

'You don't need to,' she said. 'It all fits—your motives, your playing honeymoons with me since you married me because I was—handy, and the classic "other woman" waiting in the wings——' She had stopped there, because in two strides he stood over her, a hand hard on each of her shoulders, dangerously close to her throat.

'And so,' he rasped angrily, 'think that, chew on it, and enjoy the meal! When you come to your senses we *may* talk, though you'll get nothing from me under threat. Meanwhile I'll leave you to it. If you're of the same view by midnight, don't wait up for me, for I shall be late. I might decide to make a night of it, at that. Or even more——'

With which he had flung her roughly from him. She had seen him snatch up his valise from the hall, had heard the outer door open and slam, the sound a knell to her hope that he could have dispelled all her fears with a word. A word of denial of the scurrility, an easy laughing-off of 'darling' to that other girl.

But he hadn't offered her either; he had left her instead, and who knew when—or even whether —he meant to come back?

She had known that she couldn't bear to wait —perhaps in vain—to see whether he did or not. But her movements after that were a blur in her memory. She only knew that she had packed a bag with bare necessities and had written him a note, giving him a *Poste Restante* address in England. But of her journey and arrival in Harwich, the Essex town where she had spent her childhood, she had little recollection. She had gone to a small hotel while she searched for and found the one-room flat which had become her home for five years—and Luc had written to the address she had given him.

He was leaving Menton immediately, he wrote. He appended the name and address of his solicitors. If she wanted to reach him she could do so through them, and meanwhile, if she would furnish them with a firm address for herself, he would arrange for maintenance to be paid to her through them.

She had never written to them.

Somehow she got through what should have been a pleasant meal with the Marlowes. Richard told how, when he had retired from eighteen years in the Merchant Navy, he had been depressed by the rat-race promised by civilian life. But he had been fortunate in getting in touch with Luc within a year of Luc's project for the neglected southern coast of Corsica having been under way.

Corsica? Had moving here always been in Luc's mind? Cleo wondered. She knew he was familiar with it, having spent his summers in the island as a boy, and now Richard was confirming Luc's plans.

'He envisaged a resort that would be remote enough to deter the hordes on the Riviera, yet be accessible enough by air and sea to attract the people who would take trouble to enjoy their sun and their scenery and their yachting in peace,' Richard said.

'It must have needed a good deal of—capital?' Cleo suggested carefully.

'Initially, yes,' Richard agreed. 'But the Corsican banks cottoned on to the idea, knowing the island needed development, and Luc has charm and persuasion enough to coax funds from a Swiss financial gnome.'

(But he would have had money to show to the banks in the first place.) Aloud Cleo asked, 'Do you always call Monsieur Vidame "Luc"?'

It was Anne who answered that with a laugh. ' "Luc" when we're all boys and girls together, "the Director" on grand occasions, and "the Big Man" when we want to imply that it's he who has the last word. And you'll be "Cleo" to everyone, if that's all right with you?'

'Of course,' Cleo said, despising her cowardice for having accepted even one meal from these kind people, instead of facing them at once with the truth of her duplicity. Tomorrow. She must tell them she couldn't stay, tomorrow. She couldn't blurt it out tonight.

They took her back to their villa for coffee, and Richard saw her to her chalet after dark.

She undressed at once, envying the expectant mood in which she had been able to unpack before she had gone down to the office. She slipped a filmy matching robe over her nightgown and was doing her hair at the miniature toilet-table in the shower room when she was surprised by a knock on the door from the balcony to the living-room which was her 'front' door.

She went to it a little fearfully. Who could want her at night? Indeed, who knew she was there but the Marlowes? But of course! It could be one of them needing to tell her something. She opened—to Luc standing on the threshold. Luc, expressionless, cold.

She made to shut the door on him, but his foot went to it. 'You—you can't come in,' she quavered. 'N-not here. *Please*——!'

She saw his glance flick to the daybed which she had made ready for sleeping. 'And who with more right to come into your bedroom than I?' he parried, and came in. Lifting her hand off the door-handle, he shut it and leaned back on it, arms folded.

'Don't worry,' he said. 'Nobody saw me, so no one will tell on you, and there is no neighbour near enough to hear you, if you set up any virgin-about-to-be-ravished alarm. Meanwhile, *Miss Tyndall*, you and I have to talk.'

CHAPTER TWO

CLEO backed away, one hand at her throat, the other holding her robe edge to edge. Luc watched her until the backs of her knees touched the day-bed, when he advised coolly, 'You shouldn't sit there if you think you're in danger of assault. You might find a chair safer,' and hooked one towards her with his foot.

She took it. He remained standing, hands now in slacks' pockets. She found herself remembering and loving every movement he made, every inflection of his voice, however cruel his words. She looked up at him in appeal, but his watchfulness of her held nothing but a steely appraisal which left her naked of confidence, naked of hope.

She found her voice. 'You knew——all along?'

He understood the mental shorthand behind the question. 'But of course,' he said. 'The "Cleone Tyndall" of the signature to your letter to the Marlowes was no disguise for your photograph. In fact'——he made an insult of the phrase ——'I'd have known you anywhere!'

She flinched. 'And yet you let me come!'

'Why not? You were the best of the bunch of

27

the applicants. I looked forward to your arrival as a piquant situation, and I confess to a mild curiosity as to what the years might have done to you—or for you.'

She was hungry to know how she looked to him now, but she scorned to ask and was totally unprepared for his stepping forward to tilt her face up to his scrutiny under the light.

'M'm,' he mused. 'Much as I expected—you wear well, as your untouched gamine type does —eyes as outwardly trusting as a spaniel's; dewy lips asking to be kissed, and claws neatly hidden until you scent injury, real or imagined, when—— Wow!' He grimaced and let her go.

She began to plead, 'If I did only imagine injury, Luc——' But she might not have spoken.

'Why "Tyndall"?' he demanded. 'Wasn't "Madame Vidame" good enough for you? And where did you run to when you left me for unknown parts?'

She said, 'I went back to Harwich—you know, where I'd lived before I joined Aunt Olive in Menton. There were people who knew me there, and it was easier to get back as Cleo Tyndall than to—explain. Especially since I was as alone as when I'd left.'

'And what have you been doing ever since?'

'I told the Marlowes in my letter; I got a job as a purser's assistant on the day and night boats running to the Hook of Holland. I kept a bed-sitting room in Harwich and was able to use it when I got back from the day-run. On the night-run I had quarters on board.'

'And no doubt collected a cosy social circle of Merchant Navy types. You and Richard will be able to compare notes about the delights of life on the ocean wave!'

That roused her. 'Of course I made friends— went about with them. In the whole of five years, what do you expect—that I would have shut myself in a cell like a nun?'

He shrugged. 'The very last thing I'd have expected, since you were posing as single and therefore open to suggestion—honourable or otherwise. I'd be a fool to suppose any marriage vows you had made to me had deterred you from having yourself a ball.'

'There's been nothing like that for me,' she denied indignantly. 'Nothing!'

'Currently, probably not, or you couldn't have assured the Marlowes, hand on heart, that you had left no entanglements behind you. But what about your commitment to me—how do you propose to explain that?'

She stared at him. 'But I shan't have to! I can't stay, after this. Since I've deceived them so far into thinking we don't know each other, I shall have to give them some other reason for my leaving. But leave I must! And now you've had your "piquant situation" at my expense, *you* can't want me to stay either.'

'Though if you think I am going to stand by while you add lie on lie to Richard and Anne, you are mistaken. You came in the false pretence that you had no commitments, and that alone puts you under an obligation which you've no right to disclaim. They had a great deal of trouble finding someone suitable for the job. You filled the bill perfectly; they seem to have taken to you, and as Anne finds herself placed, I'm going to insist that you honour your contract to the letter.'

Cleo bit back hot protest. ' "As Anne is placed"?' she queried instead.

'She hasn't told you that she is three months pregnant?'

'But——?'

Luc evidently read her thought. 'Yes, she is forty-three and could be at some risk. But they are both desperate for a child, and the idea and the special importance of you was—is—that when the time comes, you should be capable of sharing some management with Richard. You see?'

'If—if I stay.'

'You are staying,' he said crisply. 'That's final.'

She protested then, 'How can I? It'll be an impossible scene! We shall have to meet, talk, pretend——'

'Only to a common celibacy, which shouldn't be too difficult. And I must say I can hardly wait to see you in your vestal virgin's role again.'

Forcing herself to ignore that, she took him up on 'celibate'. 'You mean you've let the Marlowes —your friends here—believe you're not married?' she asked.

'With no wife in evidence, why not?' he countered. 'After all, it makes for a certain freedom, as you admit you've found.'

'You too, of course. What did I expect?' she flashed. And then, 'That woman you were telephoning—that day in Menton? *Did* you meet her in Paris, as you arranged?'

'Not that it's any business of yours after all this time, but yes, I did.' There was no mercy in either his look or his tone.

'And you saw her again after that?'

'Several times.'

'And the business you had in Paris? That was to arrange about the—the money? And with it you were able to set up—all this?' The wave of her hand indicated the estate.

'Considering how you've washed your hands of my affairs, even to complete independence of me, isn't that even less of your business?' he enquired. And then, 'End of interrogation session, hm?'

She gave in, deflated. 'I refuse to press you,' she said.

'Good. Then we understand each other so far, and you will have to put up with seeing me around.' He continued to scrutinise her, rocking slightly on his heels. 'As a matter of interest, what did you expect when you found me at your door?'

'Expect? Why, nothing. I—just didn't think you should have come,' she answered bewilderedly.

'Hope for, then, when you opened the door to me and realised I meant to come in?'

'Hope for? What do you mean?'

'Just enquiring whether you thought I had come to kiss and make up, open-armed and welcoming, breathing something corny like "At last!" No?'

She stared at him. 'After your denial of me in front of the Marlowes? *Expect* anything of you? *Hope* for anything, but what I've got, and the pitifully little I realise now I ever had? No!'

Luc remained unmoved by the quiver in her voice. 'Just as well,' he said. 'For nothing was further from *my* mind than to beg any favours or to offer them. If I'd wanted them, as the law stands at present, I'd have had the right to take them. But I don't happen to want them just now, thank you very much.'

But as he turned on his heel after that insolence, suddenly Cleo found new spirit.

She said, 'Just a minute. You said you were

curious as to what our years apart have done for me? Well, I'll tell you. I've grown up in them. I've learned how not to need—a man. How to forget what you did to me, and how to forgive what you've said to me tonight——'

'*Forgive?* And who is the forgiver and who the forgiven?' He had turned again, flaring, and was standing over her. 'So you did think you were going to offer me the hand of mercy? And perhaps you'd like the amnesty sealed with a loving kiss? Well——?'

He suddenly lunged at her and his lips came down on hers, iron-hard and brutish, asking nothing in response. He had pinioned her upper arms, cramping the effort of her spread hands on his chest to keep distance between his body and hers. The harsh pressure of his mouth was a punishing assault, no pleasure expected of it, no pleasure given. While it lasted he was raw animal male, exerting physical dominance over despised female. It was an assertion of a power over her which she could not match. Nor—the thought raced through the turmoil of her mind—would she have wanted to deny it, if only . . . if only she could believe that beneath the insistent arrogance there was a vein of tenderness, of understanding, left for her. But there was nothing, and she could only submit, passive and helpless, until he had the will to let her go.

When he did, with an abruptness which almost

threw her off balance, she had to fight a cruel chaos of feelings which strained towards him in longing, while hating a possession of her which took what it cared to take, without wanting it at all.

With an effort she achieved enough dismissing calm to say, 'You interrupted me. I was telling you that, whatever else has happened to me, these years without you have turned me into a woman. I'm not a trusting spaniel, nor a vestal virgin any more.'

The look he turned on her was long, deep and infinitely disturbing.

'Aren't you forgetting something? *I* made you a woman,' he said.

The door slammed and she was alone.

She woke too soon to the sunshine of a morning which should have been the first of the adventure of her new job, but which she faced with dread.

The half-sleep which was all she had had during the night had fantasised the meeting with Luc into a rapturous reunion. In it he *had* held his arms wide to her; she *had* run into them, her breath sobbing in her throat at the wonder of it. Holding her, heart to heart, he had kissed her then—for love, not in brutal assertion of his power to reject her, and she had waked to the ache of sobs which were the reality of her desolation.

Fully awake at last, she lay on her back, a hand flung over her eyes, hating the light. As her mind cleared it was full of questions, the overriding one being why she had bowed to Luc's insistence that she stay to see the thing through. She had implied one lie to the Marlowes. Would they think so very much the worse of her for another one, successful enough to set her free? Luc had forbidden her to tell it, but neither he nor they could keep her here against her will. So by whose will was it that she was staying? Reluctant as she was to know it, she had to admit that it was by her own. Having found Luc again she could not, *could not* return to the desert where she had walked alone for so long. Since her fate had willed their meeting, she would bow to it for the few months of having him in her sight. But was that cowardice or courage? She did not know.

There was no one about when she got up and when she went to the restaurant for breakfast there was no one to talk to but the young Corsican waitress on duty whose French was laced with local *patois* words, but with whom she managed to communicate.

After serving Cleo's coffee and croissants the girl hovered. 'Most people take *petit déjeuner* in their chalets,' she said. 'We do not have many coming for it here.'

'Not even in high summer?' Cleo asked.

'Ah, in the season it is different. Then we have

the yachtsmen who are anxious to get afloat, leaving their wives in bed. But now the only early person who comes is Monsieur Vidame himself. He sometimes gives parties in his villa, but he doesn't do his own everyday catering there.'

Cleo caught her breath. When Anne Marlowe had said of Luc that he 'came and went', she had visualised his quarters as being in Bonifacio. 'The Director stays here in a villa, then?' she queried.

'Oh yes, most of the time from now on, though he also has an apartment in the Citadel. His villa here is on L'Allée Napoléon, not far from your chalet, mademoiselle. Have you not seen it?' The girl glanced up at a wall clock. 'Monsieur was here last night, for I saw his car quite late. So he should be here soon, and then you will be company for each other, will you not, mademoiselle?'

But with an eye on the door, Cleo refused another cup of coffee and made her escape. After last night's parting, Luc could not want to see her, any more than she was prepared to face him over a breakfast table. The waitress had told her that the estate shop where she could stock up with most things for her own catering would now be open. So she went there, passing the end of Napoléon avenue on the way, fearful lest Luc should be coming down it before she was out of sight.

When she went to the office at nine o'clock Anne was already there, prepared to be busy. She took Cleo through the filing system, the card index of guests and bookings, and explained the big wall-chart for dates and times of arrivals and departures, and the to-scale diagram of the layout of every plot on the estate. Then she produced a mailing-list and a pile of glossy brochures, which Cleo was to seal and address to each client on the list.

Anne looked at her watch. 'We've very few people coming in or leaving yet. But at eleven I have to check the inventory of one family that's going out. I'll take you with me and show you how it's done.'

The outgoing tenants of the pretty villa they visited was a French family from Lyon, who were full of enthusiasm for their stay. The making of the inventory of all the movable furniture and utensils had no problem for Cleo's trained mind, and when it was finished Madame kissed both her and Anne, declaring that never would she and Monsieur take a holiday other than at La Réserve.

Back at the office Anne was instructing Cleo to go over to the kitchens to rustle up the cleaning women to take over at the French family's chalet in an hour's time, when Luc came in.

'Dilemma,' he said to Anne. 'Rachel and I are making our case for the loan for the marina extension, and we are meeting this evening to put it into written shape. But her clerk has gone sick, and we'll need a typist.'

Anne looked up from the papers she was sorting. 'Meeting where?'

'At my place in town.'

'And you want Cleo—is that it?'

Luc's glance went briefly to Cleo. 'That was the idea.'

Anne hesitated. 'Yes, well—Evening? Must it be the evening?'

'I've made the appointment. Why?'

'Just that it's only Cleo's second one here, and while we're slack she could expect to have it free. I could spare her for an hour this afternoon, if you like?' Anne offered.

'Nothing doing. Rachel can only manage the evening. Around six.'

Anne gave in. 'Oh, very well. You'll take her in and bring her back, I suppose?' She turned to Cleo. 'Sorry about this. But it's estate business and rather urgent, so I hope you don't mind?'

Cleo said, 'Of course not,' to Anne, ignoring Luc, who ignored her, even saying 'Good. I'll collect her,' as if she weren't among those present.

When he had gone she asked why Anne had made his request sound like a favour which she was free to refuse.

'Well, rather too bad, I thought, after your first day's work, to have your evening press-ganged into even more. But I'm glad you showed willing willingly. It made a good impression.'

'And supposing I hadn't shown willing willingly, what then?'

Anne laughed wryly. 'I'd guess the result would have been the same. You'd still have found yourself typing to Rachel Navarre's dictation tonight. In Luc's apartment, as planned.'

'You mean he would have made an order of it?'

'Possibly. More probably he would have worked on your concern over his lack of a typist until you found yourself begging for the privilege of helping him. He deals with opposition as if he knew it would crumble like damp clay in his hand—which it usually does. Odd,' mused Anne, 'how a man who outwardly hasn't much use for women should have his knack for sweeping them out of his path without their taking offence, and even, sometimes coming back for more of the same.'

'He doesn't care for women, you think?' Cleo asked carefully.

'Well, he hasn't married, though whether that's disillusionment over one woman, or he despises the ease with which they topple like ninepins, is anyone's guess.'

'And Rachel Navarre—is she his accountant?'

'More than that. She's also his advocate—his solicitor, that would be in England. Here, in court she's "*Maître l'avocat*", and she's the exception where he's concerned. He does think the world of her, but that's more for her professional brain, I'd say, than her sex-appeal——'

Anne broke off to answer the telephone. She listened, made sympathetic noises from time to time, and rang off after assuring her caller that she understood what was wanted and would see to it.

'Another departure—an unexpected one,' she told Cleo. 'A young American couple, the Thurlows, called urgently back to the States because Mrs T.'s father is ill. They're returning their hired car to Bonifacio this afternoon, and would like us to do the inventory in time for them to check out finally as soon as they get back. I said we would handle it, but——' Anne tapped her chin thoughtfully with her ballpoint—'I've got an appointment I must keep in town, so that means you—could you manage it alone, do you think? You could? Good girl! The villa will be locked, but I'll give you a master key to it. It's just off the main drive. Look, I'll show you where on the chart.'

The office closed for two hours at noon. Cleo went back to her chalet for a luncheon of tuna fish salad which she ate on her balcony in the sun. Richard had taken over from Anne when she returned to collect the key to the Thurlows' villa and the clipboard of the items she had to check.

She found the place and was about to use the key on the door when she checked to a shrill but imperative 'Hi!' which made her start.

She turned to face a boy of about ten who came round the side of the house, treading the ground hobbyhorse-wise, astride a mini-bicycle.

'Hi,' he said again. 'Who are *you*?'

'My name is Cleo Tyndall,' Cleo smiled.

'Well, mine's Eddie Thurlow Junior. But why were you trying to get into our villa? Mom and Pop have gone into town, but they said I wasn't to let *any* stranger in—not any!'

'Very well—that was very sensible of them. But I'm not exactly a stranger. You see——'

'Well, I've never seen you before, so that makes you a stranger to me, doesn't it?'

Irrefutable as this argument was, Cleo tried again. 'But your parents were expecting me.' She tapped her clipboard. 'To make a list of all the things which belong to us, and which you'll be leaving behind, you know?'

But Eddie would have none of it. 'They said to expect Mrs Anne or Mr Richard, not you. And I'm not letting you go in, so there!' he defied.

'Oh, all right.' Cleo gave up. It meant a return to the office and an appeal to Richard, but as she stepped on to the main drive a car overtook her and pulled up.

'Where are you going? May I drop you any-where?' It was Luc who spoke from the driving-seat.

'No, thank you. I've only to go back to the office, and then come back here again,' she told him.

He glanced at the Thurlows' villa. 'There? What's the trouble, if any?'

She hesitated, reluctant to admit even so trivial a failure to him. He prompted her with an impatient 'Well?' before she said, 'It's nothing really. Anne Marlowe had deputed me to do my first inventory alone, but I've been worsted by a small boy who won't let me into his parents' villa because he doesn't know me.'

'The Thurlow boy? Well, that figures, if he's been left in charge and told not to admit anyone strange, which you are. Are the Thurlows leaving, then?'

'Yes. They rang the office this morning to ask for the inventory to be done while they had to be out. But if I can't get in——'

Luc was getting out of the car. '——or argue successfully with a ten-year-old's logic, I'd better bring up the big guns,' he said. 'Force a bridge-head for you.'

Eddie was still on the villa's tiny lawn, still astride the bike, feet firmly planted, arms folded. Luc greeted him, 'Hi! You know me?'

'Yessir. You're Mr Luc, the Big Man.'

'Right in one. And this lady is Girl Friday.'

Eddie's look at Cleo was withering. 'Huh? That so? Then she doesn't know her own name. She told me it was Cleo something. And anyway, Friday is a day of the week. It isn't a name.'

'No? Never heard of Man Friday, then?' Luc asked.

They watched Eddie struggle with his memory. Then light dawned. 'Oh—*Man* Friday? Robinson Crusoe's guy—yep,' he agreed. 'He turned up from nowhere to help Robinson on his island.'

'Just so. Same with Girl Friday here. You could say she turned up on *this* island from—almost— nowhere. And as it was Mrs Anne who asked her to come, I'm sure your pop would say it's all right to let her in.'

Eddie made a last stand. 'Oh, O.K., if you say so. But she shouldn't tell people her name is something it isn't. She's just a phoney, that's what!'

Rightly or wrongly, Cleo read a world of satiric meaning into Luc's glance her way before he murmured, 'Out of the mouths of babes and sucklings'—and then nodded towards the bike. 'Can you ride that thing?' he asked Eddie.

Eddie hesitated. 'Well, I don't balance so good all the time.'

'Care for a hand on the back of the saddle?'

'Uh-huh. But I *can* go, once you've started me. You'll see——'

'On your way, then. Round the block while Girl Friday does her stuff.'

Cleo watched Luc steadying the wobbling progress down to the road and away, aware of the ache at her heart for the glimpse he had given her of the Luc she had loved and married; Luc who knew so well how to manage people, Luc, the pet of market-women, waiters and taxi-drivers, Luc the adored playmate of the children on the Menton shore, as easy with them as he had been with Eddie Thurlow Junior; the Luc she had wanted to father her children—but who had now turned enemy, who had bought success with the money to which their marriage had helped him, and who could stoop to the barbed cruelty of that aside to her in front of the boy.

He had taken up 'phoney' and used it against her, meaning it to hurt. There were two Lucs now. One who existed only in her memory; the other, hard, alien, cruel, whom her love, tenacious but utterly bewildered, did not even know.

His return with Eddie, now pedalling boldly alone, coincided with her finishing her work in the house. He and the boy parted with a casual, 'See you,' and Luc was left with her.

She forced herself to thank him for his help, but he shrugged. 'Merely a bit of inspired finesse,' he disclaimed.

'It worked.'

'One learns to make diplomacy work. You

might have beaten the deadlock yourself, if you'd used a bit of it.'

'I'm afraid I'm rather short on diplomacy.'

He agreed coolly, 'You said it, I didn't. Like most women, for you black is black and white white, and an unashamed grey is a dirty word.'

She thought that out. 'If you mean I have standards, yes, I have.'

'Exactly. Standards as rigid as beanpoles, which give you the right to judge, without granting a hearing to the accused.'

She turned to him in appeal. 'Luc, please——! That's all over. I'm older and a different person now. So are you——'

'Rubbish. You'll be claiming next that you're wiser too, which I very much doubt.'

'Though I think you consider *you* are.'

'In dealing with your sex, yes, I am,' he stated with flat conviction.

She corrected sadly, 'I'd say rather that you were born wise—about women. At any rate you knew exactly how to charm me.'

'More rubbish, that,' he scoffed. 'When I met you, you were only too ready to be charmed.'

'And used and deceived?'

'I deceived you in nothing. You had the truth in answer to every question you asked me.'

'You admitted the truth. You had to, in face of the proof I had.'

'And you refused to accept it, walked out, and

after chewing on your grievance all this time, now have the nerve to whinny "Forgive and forget." Black! Whiter than white! Standards! You can keep them, and leave me to wallow in my slough of grey, which will be a deal more comfortable than a halo of rectitude, earned with a "confession" of guilt!' he stormed.

'I——'

But he had got into his car and was staring ahead, ignoring her. When after a moment he said, 'I'll call for you at five-thirty this evening. Be ready, please,' he did not even look at her.

The Luc she didn't know now and she would never know again drove away.

When he arrived for her she did not keep him waiting for longer than it took her to join him in the car.

Presently he said, 'You realise of course that this is one of our public appearances; in other words, not an occasion for verbal fisticuffs, like last night's and this afternoon's?'

'Of course,' she said, and then with a touch of spirit, 'You can take it that as far as I'm concerned, *all* our appearances together in future can be public ones which anyone is free to witness.'

He nodded. 'Good. Then you can begin by thinking twice before you look for trouble with provocative speeches like that.' He paused. 'I hear you were at breakfast in the restaurant this morning, and though Lydie told you she was expecting me, you didn't wait.'

'I didn't particularly want to see you this morning—after last night.'

'Nor I you—daisy-fresh and radiating magnanimity. But it could have had the makings of an appearance prosaic enough to fool anybody. You could have poured my coffee, passed me the butter. We could have discussed the headlines in the paper. I should have enquired whether you'd slept well, and you would have replied with some cliché about as soon as your head having touched the pillow——'

Cleo flinched. 'Don't, please,' she begged. 'I've told you I'm prepared to behave in public exactly as you want, and I will. But don't make it sound as if it were some game we're playing, for it's not.'

'Game or not, it has moves and rules which you'll need to abide by, if you're going to hang on to some kind of dignity and keep Anne's and Richard's regard for you.'

'I know that.'

Silence fell and Luc's next remark was to point out the beach to which there was a short cut on foot from the estate, and then the marina of which two mooring-bays were complete, a third under construction. 'In the season we can easily fill all three,' he said.

The road up to the old town from the port was

a cobbled ramp, an ever-present threat to the car's springs. Luc's apartment was in a narrow street of houses which still had traces of their mediaeval origins, arcaded at street level and each first-floor window under a pointed arch like an individual eave. There should have been a magnificent view from that height, but the Citadel rock overhung the port, and out to sea an evening heat-haze had blotted out Sardinia. Luc's concierge greeted him in Corsican patois; he replied in French and led the way up to the first floor.

He opened a heavy oak door on to a room which was obviously part living-room, part study. The oak chairs were severely functional, only a couple of them cushioned. There was a table and a shelved dresser, and a big desk holding a type-writer and piles of papers.

He pointed to the typewriter. 'It's a French keyboard. Can you manage it?'

'Yes. You remember——' Cleo caught herself up. She would *not* remind him of the past. 'That is, I've often used one before,' she finished instead.

She could have spared herself the scruple. 'That would be when you were maid-of-all-work to your aunt, I suppose?' he asked indifferently.

'In Menton, yes.' But she spoke abstractedly, her attention taken by something on the desk—the paperweight holding down one of the paper piles, a paperweight that was a glass swan on a pearly lake. She knew he was watching her, but she could not resist touching the swan's head with a forefinger.

Time rolled back . . . She was in a Menton apartment, a gift-wrapped parcel held behind her back. 'Guess?' she had teased, and had passed the parcel into her left hand when he had snatched at her right, then caught her round the waist instead, drawing her to him, his whole will and body alive, she had known, to the sensual pleasure of imprisoning her, daring her to break free of the rain of kisses, random on throat, lips, hair, nose-tip, until suddenly the joke was over, turned to an engulfing tide of passion to which they had surrendered, lost to all but the ecstasy of their desire.

Time adjusted itself, levelled out to bleak Now. She heard Luc saying evenly, 'Strange, isn't it, how inanimate things keep their beauty and their use when human relationships don't?' Then he looked out of the window. 'Rachel Navarre,' he said and went down to meet her.

He brought her up and introduced Cleo to her. She looked to be in her late thirties; dressed in severe black, tall with strong aquiline features, black hair drawn into a tight chignon on her nape. Her handshake for Cleo was as firm as a man's. Her eyes were deep-set beneath too-heavy brows. The woman of whom, according to Anne Marlowe, Luc 'thought the world' was no physical beauty, but she had poise and a presence which commanded notice. And she was about Luc's present age—— Was it possible, Cleo wondered with a stab of jealousy, that she could have been the '*mignonne*' he had been talking to in that fatal telephone call? He had seen that girl since, he had admitted last night. How long had he known Rachel Navarre?

She thanked Cleo pleasantly for standing in for her clerk, and she and Luc got down to the business in hand, discussing in French technical questions which Cleo did not understand. She sat listening until they had agreed on and drafted some letters for her to type. Rachel dictated them to her and congratulated her on their execution. Luc produced drinks, cognac and *pastis*. He drank cognac himself and poured the clear gold of the *pastis* for Rachel and Cleo.

It was a drink that was new to Cleo. She watched it turn to a cloudy grey when he swirled water into it, and she sipped it experimentally, while the other two continued to talk shop.

Then Rachel changed the subject. 'There was a case of *attacar* in the town this morning,' she remarked.

Luc seemed to understand her. 'So? Who?' he asked.

'The man? One of the Cirneos.'

'And the girl?'

'Marguerite Clouson. He waylaid her on the

quay, snatched off her headscarf and flicked her in the face with it. I hear the Clousons are rabid to bring him into court, but that's no solution, as they well know. He didn't assault the girl or do her an injury, except in the eyes of her family, and to the satisfaction of his. It's just one more step in the feud between the Cirneos and the Clousons, and there's no law that they recognise against carrying it on. Now it's up to the Clousons to think up the next move to avenge poor Marguerite.' Rachel turned to Cleo. 'You wouldn't understand this, would you, if you don't know Corsica?' she asked.

'It sounds like some kind of vendetta between families,' Cleo said.

'And that's what it is, though it rarely runs to blood-vengeance or murder nowadays. One family may deeply offend another——very often through the infidelity of a man or woman, married to a member of the other, and the whole family of the injured party takes up the cause and the law into their own hands. To the Corsicans, marriage is sacred and for ever——'

Luc lifted his glass and looked straight at Cleo over the rim of it. 'In other words, a marriage is a marriage is a marriage, you understand?' he taunted in English.

She withdrew her eyes from his. 'Yes,' she said, and asked Rachel, 'And then the feud is on?'

'Yes, with every insult or discredit either side

can devise. It doesn't draw blood, but it can ruin homes and break reputations at its worst. Another reason for it could be trespass, or alleged theft, or quite a common one is alleged seduction of a girl by a man.'

'And this incident this morning? The—word you used for it?'

'The *attacar*—Corsican for the contemptuous claiming of a woman. He doesn't want her, but a kiss or a touch, even of only something she's wearing, is the supreme insult to her in public, and it will be a long time before Marguerite Clouson lives it down. Another man won't be seen with her until this particular quarrel between the families has been patched up.'

'You're a primitive lot, you Corsicans,' Luc remarked without accusation.

'We do take honour and loyalty to bizarre and even dangerous lengths,' Rachel agreed. 'But our marriages last. They don't break up over trivialities; they hold fast by their roots.' She stood up. 'I must go. I have a case to prepare for court tomorrow.'

They all went down to the street together. Luc and Rachel parted with a touch, cheek to cheek. He saw her to her car and joined Cleo in his own.

'Does Madame Navarre live up here?' she asked him.

'Call her Rachel. You'll see quite a bit of her.

No—down in the port with her father. She's not married.'

'From what she said, she is Corsican, not French?'

'Corsican from generations back. She studied law in Paris, practised there for a time and then came back here.'

'I see.' Dare she ask more? Dates, for instance? How he and Rachel Navarre had met? How well they had known each other in Paris? Or even why Rachel had returned to practise in the island? Because Luc had then been here? Or could she hope that he had guessed the drift of her questions and would be merciful enough to spare her any more doubts?

She waited, venturing a furtive glance at his fine-cut profile. But he continued to stare ahead at the road, withdrawn from her, evincing no memory of a telephone call in which he had welcomed his *mignonne* to Paris, promising to meet her there . . .

He was not going to help, and she would *not* beg it of him. Sheer pride would choke the words in her throat.

Instead of driving her to her chalet, he stopped the car outside the restaurant. To the question she looked at him he said, 'You haven't eaten. We'll dine here.'

'I hadn't meant to. I'd prepared some supper for myself.' But she resisted in vain. With a hand firmly under her elbow he said, 'Another public appearance. Anne and Richard will probably be eating here. They'll expect me to give you dinner, and a foursome will be good discipline for us both.'

Cleo gave in then. With the promise of the Marlowes' company there was safety in numbers, and there was temptation to being with Luc a little longer, being free to watch him, hear his voice, remember him as he was when she had believed he was hers. Even in a storm of anger and contempt of her, he would not come to her chalet tonight, and it was going to be a lonely place

CHAPTER THREE

THERE were more people at the bar than there were in the restaurant, but Anne and Richard were among the few, and Luc showed Cleo to their table. Anne, patting a chair for Cleo, said, 'We usually eat here at night before the season begins. When it does, there's no battling with the crowds. How did you get on?'

For Cleo the hour spent over the meal was a relaxing one. Luc's manner towards her was as detached as any employer's; Anne was her friendly self and Richard and Luc were mostly engrossed in discussing estate business. They lingered on over their coffee and were the last of the restaurant's patrons to leave their table. Outside, claiming she wanted a walk, Anne suggested that she and Richard would see Cleo home on foot, relieving Luc of the necessity to drive her.

Inwardly Cleo welcomed the offer. She had been dreading a tête-à-tête parting from Luc at her door and had been ready to say goodnight to the three of them and to leave alone. She told Anne, 'That would be kind.' Luc said coolly, 'As you please.' Richard asked him if he were stay-

ing at his villa for the night. He said he was, and
went to his car.

Anne linked arms with Cleo and with her husband. 'Well, obviously you couldn't say in front
of him, but how do you think you and Luc are
going to click?' she asked Cleo.

'When I was young, the verb "to click" meant
to achieve a sexual success,' Richard put in.

Anne shook his arm playfully. 'Oh, you——!
You're hopelessly out of date anyway. The current word is "score". No, Cleo knows very well
that I'm asking how she thinks she'll find working for him. Don't you?' she appealed to Cleo.

'Shall I be working for him—directly?' Cleo
asked carefully.

'Well, no more than for Richard and me. But
he *is* the boss and more than a bit of a perfec-
tionist, expecting so much of you that you tend
to feel an awful heel if you let him down.'

'Is that why you let him get round you as you
do?' Richard asked.

Anne dimpled at him. 'It's easier than arguing,
when you know he'll get his way, and he knows
that you know! But Cleo won't have sized him
up yet, and I'm wondering what she's made so
far of that assumption of his that the gods had
better be on his side—or else!'

Since something was expected of her, Cleo
said, 'If he does assume that, it seems to have
brought him a good way. But I think I'm going to

find him a difficult person to know. Much more
so than you are, for instance. You've both welcomed me——'

'Ah well,' Anne beamed, 'that's because we like
people, as people. *Really* like them—as I doubt
if Luc does. He can charm them so easily, and
knows it, that he doesn't have to bother to
like them too, or care whether they like him. One
wouldn't know whether he's always been that
way, or whether, as I said to you this morning,
something—or somebody—had jolted him into
it. What do you think?' she added to Richard.

Richard said, 'I think you're an imaginative
wench with an outsize yen for putting your
friends under a microscope, in order to watch
their finer wheels go round.'

'Only because I'm interested, and because I
want the people *I* like to like each other!'

'In other words, wheels within wheels,' capped
Richard, inviting a laugh.

Cleo said goodnight to them at the bottom of
the short path leading to her chalet. She left
them, feeling she had betrayed an essential part
of her love for Luc by claiming that he was difficult to know. She shouldn't have said that of
him—of the man with whom she had briefly
shared the sweet intimacy of mind and body
which, in her innocence, she had thought only a
deeply-felt union could possibly know. But
caution had driven her to it. She had had to sound

non-committal about him at this stage. And what, she wondered bleakly, would *he* say of *her*, if Anne's kindly analysis probed him about her? Cleo would have given a lot to know.

Everywhere was very quiet. When they had left the restaurant it had been about to close, and soon the whole estate would be asleep. She fumbled in her bag for her key to the door of the chalet which locked automatically on shutting. Here the key was—no, that was her pencil torch. Her *key*—where was it? A less hasty search revealed that it was not in her bag, and suddenly she remembered having put it on the table when she had last used it. It must still be there. There was only one door to the chalet, and she was locked out.

She sighed. What to do? She would have to follow Anne and Richard down to their villa near the entrance, and ask their help. She ought to be able to catch them up. She set out at a run.

But either they had walked very fast or had detoured for a longer stroll by the light of the moon which was riding high, pursued by cotton-wool clouds, for she had not come up with them by the time she reached the swimming-pool at about the central point of the estate. Thinking to give the other two time to get home if they had gone by a longer way, she paused by the pool, expecting its water to be still and dark, except for the reflected path of the moon on its surface.

But it was ruffled, and busily astir, with wave-
lets rippling and clapping on the poolsides—the
noisy displacement caused by something cleaving
through the water at speed. Some eccentric was
swimming there. At this time of night? Cleo
moved into the shadow of a dressing-cabin to
watch the swimmer's arrow-straight progress
from pool-end to pool-end in an expert racing
crawl. Luc used to swim like that . . . At the far
end, at his turn, the man lifted his head in full
moonlight. It *was* Luc—the last person to whom
she wanted to excuse her foolish plight. There
wasn't time to step out of the shadow and escape
while he did his next length towards her, but if
she stayed where she was until he turned
again——

So much for plans. Reaching her end, he
climbed out, swept back his hair with both hands
and padded to where his towel and short gown
hung on a pole within arm's length of where Cleo
stood. Only by a miracle could he not see her, and
he did. What was more, he did not wait for her
to move towards him, but reached out a wet hand
and jerked her out with a circular turn of his
wrist which brought her up so close to the gleam-
ing bronze of his torso that he might have been
swinging her into his embrace.

In her nostrils was the once-familiar fresh smell
of his skin after swimming; close under her eyes
were the sparkling droplets which had beaded on

his chest; one small invitation from his hands or hers, and they could be in each other's arms ...

He threw her wrist from him. 'What are you doing here?' he demanded. 'I thought the Marlowes were to see you home?'

'And they did.'

'Well?' He was tying the sash of his robe and thrusting his feet into heelless sandals. For all the warmth in his tone she might have been a suspected character caught out after curfew.

She said, 'I've locked myself out—left my key inside—and I was following them to their villa to ask Richard's help. Then I noticed someone was swimming and——'

'You saw that *I* was swimming?'

'I wasn't spying on you or pursuing you!' she denied indignantly. 'I thought you'd gone to your own villa.'

'I had. But when I stay the night here, I like to swim after dark—and alone.' He went on, 'About your key—there's no need to disturb Anne and Richard now. I can get a passkey from the office, but I shall have to go back to my own place to fetch the key to that.'

Cleo moved away. 'I'll walk on down, then, and wait for you,' she said.

'You'll do no such thing. The restaurant has closed, but the bar is only shutting about now——'

'And you think I can't ignore any of its patrons who may have stayed there too long?'

'I've no doubt that your Merchant Navy service may have widened your experience of over-jolly tars on their rolling way home,' he said caustically. 'But I'm not risking a late-night assault involving any of our clients and our hired help, so you will stay with me, please, until I take you back to your own place.'

She had no choice. But she determined that if he attempted conversation on the way she would reply in monosyllables or not at all. 'Our hired help.' What a deliberate slight he had made of the words! He wasn't concerned for her, herself, but only that as an employee of his—*any* employee—she shouldn't be laid open to the kind of annoyance which might make for gossip on the estate. That was all she was to him—one of the hired help.

He showed her into his living-room, a more spacious version of her own. He said, 'You'll have to wait while I change,' and left her. When he came back he was in shirt and slacks, his hair still damp from the pool and the shower she had heard running. She had always loved to see it like that, plastered down like a schoolboy's . . .

He went to a corner cabinet, bent to it. 'A drink,' he said. 'My habit after a swim. What about you?'

'No, thank you.' She looked about her with what she hoped was a hint.

Luc nodded. 'I know—the key. All in good time.' With his drink in his hand and one foot on a chair-rung, he went on, 'As I said, I don't doubt your ability to hand the frozen mitt to any too-merry reveller who accosted you. But if he didn't understand the signals, he could make a damned nuisance of himself to you.'

Cleo said, 'I think I could cope. But had you some particular one of the residents in mind?'

'None at all. But they're men, at leisure here, relaxed. Justified, they'd argue, in spelling "female" in three letters—F. U. N. And indeed one can't blame them for chancing their arm if, rightly or wrongly, they read the red light as green.'

'And you mean to protect me—or rather, your women staff—from that kind of annoyance?'

'Exactly. And though they may think the glassy look or the scornfully hitched shoulder will get them by, I still count it as my responsibility to guard their morals on my estate.'

'Thank you,' Cleo said coldly. 'Though, do you know, I've an idea I can guard my own?'

'You think so?' He paused, allowing his glance to measure her, travelling slowly from her silver-fair hair, ruffled by the night wind, over her body, dwelling, she thought, on the thrust of her breasts, then assessing her waist and hips and her legs below the modest length of the day-dress in which she had gone to Bonifacio. Embarrassed, she stirred under his scrutiny as he went on, 'And yet you and I, admittedly on a legitimate errand, but alone here—right?'

'Y—yes.'

'And do you realise, I wonder, just how vulnerable you are? How little your disdain or your frigidly curled lip or your demure workaday clothes could protect you from me if I decided to take you—if I wanted to?'

Cleo prayed that, from his distance, her trembling wasn't visible. 'But you wouldn't want to,' she stated flatly.

'Oh, I don't know.' He studied her again. 'With that figure and that touch-me-not air, you aren't without interest to the male ego, and if you were merely a casual pick-up, we'd probably achieve a passing success, supposing I made the usual advances.'

'But you didn't pick me up because you liked the look of me. I've been your wife, and you *don't* want to touch me.'

'Ah, that certainly makes for complications.' He frowned as if faced with a genuine dilemma. 'Alters the case, doesn't it? And so——'

He paused for so long that she prompted him. 'Well——?'

'And so,' he repeated, 'isn't it lucky for you that I'm not wilfully colour-blind?'

'Not——? What do you mean?'

'That I'm not tempted to read the green of an

invitation into the red flash you're giving off, of course.'

'Because if I were—willing that you should touch me, you'd have to disappoint me, you're saying? Well, you needn't worry. *I'm* not playing coy with you. I—I wouldn't let you near me to-night for—for anything!' Cleo flared.

He sighed elaborately. 'Which is where we came in, namely that *if* I chose to exercise my conjugal rights tonight, you couldn't stop me, if only for physical reasons. But as we seem to be of one mind, we'll now go about the business that brought us.' And with what seemed to be almost a single movement he set down his glass, took a key from the top of a bureau beside him, and was opening the door for her, holding it so little ajar that she had to brush against his body to go through it. Her nerves a-quiver with longing, Cleo fell into step beside him.

As he had forecast, half a dozen men and a couple of women were leaving the bar as they passed it. They linked arms and strolled off, singing, without recognising Luc. He got the passkey from the office, then he and Cleo retraced their way back to her chalet. He unlocked the door and stood aside for her to enter. But he hadn't done with her yet. 'As a matter of interest,' he asked, 'supposing I had indeed been your hitherto un-known employer of only a few hours, would you have gone as willingly with me to my villa as you did?'

'Willingly? You told me I must!'

'Don't beg the question. This hypothetical chap, almost a stranger to you, invited you to his villa where you knew he camped alone. Did you go?'

She hesitated. 'Well, I had to have help, and his reasons for asking me sounded genuine. But no, probably not.'

'Only "probably"?' Luc pressed.

'Not, then. Why do you want to know?' (If only, if only he would tell her in reply, *Because I care that you shouldn't.*)

But all he said was, 'Just testing.'

'Testing?' Driven to asperity by her frayed nerves, 'You sound like a radio engineer! Testing *what?*' she demanded.

'My technique. Goodnight,' he said.

The week which followed was to be the last of the estate's out-of-season leisured existence. The next week led up to Whitsuntide and the summer influx of visitors began in earnest. But that first week had been Cleo's training-ground, and by the time Whitsun came, she felt she had her job well in hand. As well as the car which she would use for driving to the airport, she had been given the use of a miniature moped, enamelled a vivid fluorescent orange, on which she could get about the grounds, and which Richard had nicknamed the Yellow Peril. On this, in her own time, she had explored and noted the name of every avenue on the two-hundred-acre estate. She went down to the beach on foot and into Bonifacio by car, memorising shops and services for the information of the people who besieged the office, wanting to know where they could get their hair done, buy souvenirs or the local aromatic honey, park their cars, arrange for a day's fishing or book for an island tour.

Anne Marlowe praised, 'You really are turning into my right-hand person,' and confided her hopes of her baby in the autumn. Richard, who was fluent in it, encouraged her to speak French as often as possible, and on one occasion suggested to Luc that she should accompany him as his secretary at a meeting with his Ajaccio bank on the matter of the marina loan.

But Luc dealt shortly with that suggestion. 'No need. Rachel and her clerk will be there,' he said —only to arrive in the office early on the morning of the meeting to say that Rachel had to make an essential appearance in court and couldn't accompany him.

'So I can use Cleo if you can spare her,' he told Richard. 'Also if she's capable of following the gist and taking notes on what goes on in French.' He looked at his watch. 'The meeting is at noon, so I'd like to catch the eleven o'clock plane from

Siccone. I'll call for her here at half-past ten.'

When he had gone Cleo voiced her misgivings to Richard. 'It will all be terribly technical, won't it? That night in Bonifacio he and Rachel Navarre drafted the letters and I only had to take her dictation. But here I shall have to take down everything that's said as it's being said, and I doubt if I can,' she worried.

'You'll manage. No problem,' Richard assured her. 'Your notes will only be for Luc's use, so you can listen and translate them into English or use a mixture of both, if you like. He's bi-lingual enough himself to take in his stride whatever hotch-potch you have to produce. But a report of the proceedings he must have.'

On that journey to Ajaccio, by car to the airport, in the little plane and by taxi to the bank through the busy streets of the city, Cleo felt Luc must be congratulating himself that there was nothing to suggest their relationship was anything other than that of an executive on a business trip with his secretary. Those two nights of conflict and recrimination, neither of which she had invited, might never have happened.

On the way to Siccone he had told her that she would find Ajaccio much more sophisticated and more tourist-ridden than Bonifacio; on the way to becoming the second Riviera from which he hoped to keep La Réserve and its surroundings free. In the plane he briefed her on how the meeting might go, and in the taxi he occupied himself with his papers, ignoring her.

The meeting proved less of an ordeal than she had feared. It seemed to go well for Luc, and listening to him making his points, she was lost in admiration of the mastery of his argument. She longed for the right to be proud of him too. But that didn't belong to her any more.

They lunched with the bank directors in their boardroom, and when they came out on to the city's wide principal square Luc said, 'I've other business which will keep me until about five o'clock, so if you would care to look round, meet me here then. You might like to visit Napoleon's birthplace. It's in the old town, behind the fishing-port. A taxi would take you there, or there are the beaches, the Promenade or the shops. But please don't get lost. We have to catch the six o'clock plane back.'

Everything in Ajaccio, it seemed to Cleo, was geared to Corsica's most famous son. There were Napoleon hotels, Napoleon public gardens, Emperor bars and cafés, and Little Corporal antique and souvenir shops. She found a taxi-driver who gave her a miniature guided tour, whisking her round so that she should 'see all', allowing her only an outside view of the birthplace in favour of a bucketing ride through the narrow alleys of the port, back to the grand boulevards of luxury shops and around the great sweep of the Promen-

ade Napoléon, which showed her what Luc had
meant. Crescent-shaped, palm-lined, the site of
the city's top-star hotels, it was indeed so much
to the pattern of the Promenade des Anglais of
Nice or the Croisette of Cannes that it might have
been on the Riviera. She decided she preferred the
primitive waterfront of Bonifacio.

About an hour before she had to rejoin Luc she
asked her driver if he knew of a quiet little beach
which wouldn't be crowded. He did, he claimed,
and drove her out of the town a short way along
the coast to a cove secluded by rocks, where the
sea lapped gently on a curve of firm golden sand.
Claiming her as his profitable property for the
afternoon, he said he would come back for her in
time for her to keep her rendezvous, shook her
warmly by the hand and left her.

It was a delightful place. Cleo sat on the sand,
her back against the glowing warmth of a rock,
wishing she had been wearing a swimsuit under
her dress, as she sometimes did, in order to catch
a quick dip in the pool at lunchtime. But though
swimming was out, paddling was in, and presently she kicked off her sandals at the water's
edge and splashed along to the 'horn' of the cove
to see if she could paddle round it to find out
what lay beyond it.

But the water was too deep. She wandered back
towards the other horn, up to her calves and kick-
ing spray idly when, just short of it, a vicious

pain in her foot sent a chill throughout her blood-
stream, causing her to cry out and to collapse into
the shallow water, panting and biting her lip in
agony.

She sat, waiting for the water to redden from
a cut which could only have been inflicted by
broken glass, she was sure. But the water round
her foot remained clear, and when she moved it,
and smoothed her hand carefully over the spot
where she had stepped, there was nothing there
but the fading mark of her footprint as the ebb
worked lazily at it.

No broken glass, no jagged tin. In fact the
whole beach was virgin-clean. Then what? She
turned on to all fours, crept up on to dry sand and
laid her foot across her knee to examine it. It was
swelling now and purpling round a punctured
hole on its ball. No blood at all had been drawn,
but the puncture seemed to go deep. The pain
was still intense and there was still that chill in
her veins. She scrabbled to stand up, but she
couldn't put that foot down. Though of course
they weren't, her sandals looked to be a mile
away, and within the next ten minutes or so she
had to get back up to the road to meet her taxi-
man, not daring to wait for him to come to find
her, in case he didn't, and she would be too late
for Luc, expecting her.

She could wear only one sandal. She crossed
the sand on all fours and 'sat' up the rough stair-

way, step by step, to the wall dividing the beach from the road. Her driver was true to his promise. He was there to time, and he helped her to hop to the taxi.

He was voluble with questions. A cut? A sprain? A *hole*? And nothing to be felt on the smooth sand? Ah——! Light dawned. '*Les vives! Les méchants! Qu'ils sont des espèces du diable!*' he exclaimed in horror.

Mentally agreeing that 'they' were indeed wicked specimens of the devil, Cleo echoed '*Les vives?*'

The man explained. They were fish which burrowed in the sand and erected a spine as sharp as a spear on their backs when threatened by, for instance, a treading foot. Nasty, was his verdict. Poisonous. Madame would suffer. She should have treatment for the wound without delay.

Cleo agreed that she should. But meanwhile she had to meet Luc, hopping on one foot, which was going to humiliate her, guessing he would show scant sympathy for an accident which needn't have happened if she hadn't gone paddling barefoot on a strange shore, and which might put her out of useful action for some days.

However, she had only just got out of the taxi and was preparing to pay the fare when Luc appeared at her side. He glanced from the sandal slung over her wrist to her foot. 'What's happened? What have you done?' he asked.

'I——' But it was the driver, eyes rolling and hands expressive, who explained. As she had expected, Luc was short on spoken concern, his only remark to her being, 'I thought you'd been warned always to wear *espadrilles* on these beaches?' before he put her back into the cab and told the driver to go to the hospital.

Cleo protested, 'We shall miss the six o'clock plane.'

'Then we'll catch the eight o'clock. You must have the wound dressed and a shot of antibiotics. So put your leg on the seat and keep it there,' Luc ordered, and got in beside the driver.

For some reason—vaguely she wondered if it were the injection she was given in the casualty ward—Cleo was hazy about the journey from the hospital to the airport and the short flight to Siccone. She thought she had been taken to the plane in a wheelchair, she slept on the flight and there was another wheelchair to take her to Luc's car.

But wheelchairs didn't just *happen*. They had to be ordered for invalids—which meant that Luc must have phoned ahead. Ungrateful of her, she thought dazedly, to feel that for just one word from him that he cared she was in pain and wasn't blaming her for causing so much trouble, she would gladly have crawled to and from the aircraft and again from his car to her chalet when they arrived.

Though if he were kind enough to pity her, he

wouldn't let her crawl, would he . . .? She pursued that thought through a fog of longing and self-pity until the stopping of the car jerked her back to reality.

She looked about her. 'Why?' she asked, as Luc alighted and came round to her side of the car.

'Why the Marlowes' place, not yours? Because they have a spare room and you aren't sleeping alone tonight,' he said. 'Come——'

Deftly he slipped one arm beneath her knees, the other round her shoulders and lifted her out, holding her close as he balanced her weight and set off up the steep path which led to the villa.

On their wedding night he had carried her into his apartment. Like this, her head in the hollow of his shoulder, her body then soft and willing and aware; her body now no more to him than a burden he was carrying from here to there. She had believed then there had been tenderness in his encircling arms, an excitement which matched her own in the quickened beat of his heart. But had there been—ever? Any more than there was now? Now his cradling was a dutiful saving of her pain, the pounding of his heart only the result of exertion.

Supposing, when he put her down, as he would have to after the next short minute or the next, she turned back into his arms, drew him to her and let her eyes, lips and hands tell him all that she wanted him to know? But of course she would not. She flinched from the thought of the repulse she would invite. He wouldn't believe her. He wouldn't *try* to believe her. There was no way of getting through to him now; it was too late.

In a few strides more he had reached the villa's sun balcony where Anne and Richard were sitting over their evening drinks. Anne and Richard and another figure—a man who set aside his glass and stepped forward as Luc put Cleo down, supporting her on her sound foot with an arm behind her shoulder.

She clung to his jacket for balance and stared at the newcomer in dazed surprise. 'Why, Bruce———!' she said—and fainted.

CHAPTER FOUR

DURING the three days before Cleo was walking normally again no one could have been kinder than Anne.

She knew '*vives*' as 'weevers' in English and blamed herself for not having warned Cleo against them on Mediterranean beaches. 'The puncture they make is nothing after the first stab of pain,' she explained. 'It's the poison they send into your blood which does the damage, and it was that, and the antidotes you'd been given, which made you faint, though Luc would have it that it was the sight of your friend. After we'd put you to bed, he even cornered the poor boy and wanted to know why!'

Her heart sinking a little, Cleo asked, 'I hope Bruce denied that it could have been?'

'Of course. He told Luc you might have been surprised to see him; you certainly couldn't have been shocked. But do you know what Luc said— pretty unforgivably—to that?'

'No?' Cleo queried faintly.

'He said, "Couldn't she—if one of the conditions of our employing her was that she could assure us she was completely free to give her whole attention to the job?" Which he, Luc, meant to demand that you had left no particular boy-friend behind you. And that being so, mightn't Bruce's arrival have been a shock?'

Cleo's fingers went nervously to her lips. 'And what did Bruce say to that?'

Anne laughed. 'The gist of it, I gather, was "So what?" He said he was the Radio Officer on board one of your North Sea ships; he had a fancy to spend his leave here, looking you up, and though he'd claim you were one of his favourite girls, you weren't engaged, and even if you were, what the so-and-so had your private life to do with your job?'

'And Luc——?'

'Snapped, "Everything, in this case, where I made the stipulation and Miss Tyndall claimed she understood it," ' and stalked off.

'Implying that I'd lied,' Cleo said wretchedly.

'As I shall tell him,' Anne claimed. 'Ask him if he imagined a pretty girl like you didn't have a lot of hopeful boys queueing up—— But now settle down, and get all the sleep you can, and we'll let friend Bruce see you in the morning.'

That had been Anne's last visit to her before she and Richard went to bed themselves, and fortunately Cleo's drug-induced sleep did its work well. She woke to little pain and a clearer head, and was sitting on the balcony when Bruce came bounding up the path to join her.

She had always liked him, but he meant no more to her than any other of the men with whom she had been on easy friendly terms in her male-predominated job. He was short and thick-set with an open freckled face and curling ginger hair, and the wry thought struck her that if Luc had any conception of his own physical attraction, he could hardly suppose that, once having loved him, she could want to make Bruce Howard a greater importance to her life. But of course Luc didn't see Bruce as a rival; his veto on Bruce or on any other man for her arose solely from his thirst for revenge.

In answer to her question Bruce explained, 'No, I didn't write for a booking here. I just arrived—by sea to Ajaccio—and told them at your office that I was merely a snail with my house on my back, and if they could rent me a few square metres, I'd put up my tent on it and squat. They could, and I did, and when I looked in again to make a few discreet enquiries about you, your sweet Mrs Marlowe invited me to drinks and to supper and to wait until you showed up. So you'll have me around for a fortnight or so, but s'welp me, what a deadpan graven image of a boss you've got! And why on earth did you let him impose such impossible rules?'

Cleo excused Luc. 'He thought they were reasonable, as they wanted someone to stay on after the season and learn management. And as I wasn't engaged or—or anything, before I got here I thought they were justified and no more than a formality.'

Bruce caught her up. '*Before* you got here? Does that mean you've fallen for some hairy Corsican bandit type since?'

'No, of course not.' Cleo managed a smile. 'And Luc Vidame hasn't anything like that to pin on me until I did that stupid collapse in the very same moment of seeing you. But Anne Marlowe says you did your best to put him right on that?'

'That we were secretly married or conducting a guilty liaison? I did indeed, though whether he believed me is anyone's guess. I hinted, however, that any time *you* were willing, I was——' Bruce paused to throw Cleo a shrewd look. 'Mean to say you want to stay on so badly after the season that you've wholly given in to this "no followers allowed" lark?' he asked.

Cleo was silent, looking into the future of a job which she would love to hold and develop, yet which must be closed to her because of Luc. What was she going to say in excuse to Richard and Anne when the time came, if they wanted her to stay on, and she knew she would be letting down Anne if she left? To Bruce, waiting for her to answer, she evaded with, 'Since it hasn't been important, I haven't queried it, and I shall have to see at the end of the season how I feel—always supposing I rate being asked to stay.'

'And meanwhile His Highness assumes your private life is his to order? D'you suppose he's going to interfere with your going around with me while I'm here? Just in case I slip a ring on your finger when you're not looking? Oh well—— But tell me, when are you free?'

Cleo had to admit, 'I'm afraid that's another of the things I've agreed to. I'm an "On Call" type, like a nurse or a doctor. I jump to it, no matter when, where or how. Never free at weekends, which is our busiest time, and though I'm supposed to be off duty in the evenings, I never quite know.'

'Then I shall hang around, pulling my forelock and looking neglected until your Mrs Anne takes pity on me and sends you to my rescue,' Bruce claimed.

Cleo laughed. 'I shouldn't count on that if I were you,' she warned.

'Oh, I don't know. I think she likes me and sees me as a nice boy for you to know. Meanwhile, as soon as you can walk, you're doing an inspection tour of my tent, and until then you'll find me constantly popping up,' was Bruce's parting, little knowing the trouble he could cause her with Luc, simply through his being there with the freedom to claim her company when he chose. 'Popping up' to him was the risk of Luc's cold censure to her.

*

As soon as she was fit, she was back into routine. She wrote letters, did inventories, went on errands for Anne, drove to and from the airport, took duty at the pool—and Luc did not come near her.

She saw him once in the distance with Rachel Navarre, but for days he wasn't on the estate. Richard said there had been a hold-up over the loan for the new marina bay. Luc wanted it completed for this season's peak, intended to get it, and heads would roll, Richard opined, if it weren't forthcoming. Meanwhile he was occupied in cajoling or bullying every jack-in-office in Bonifacio.

Cleo found time to have Bruce to lunch at her chalet, and one evening Anne lent her the car, so that he could take her out to dinner in the town.

Though he claimed he had come to Corsica mainly to swim and sunbathe and to see her, she felt guilty that by staying mostly on La Réserve, he was missing the real Corsica. So that evening she ventured with the car up to the heights of the Citadel quarter, to give him the magnificent view of the Strait and Sardinia and the feel of the buildings and narrow echoing streets of a walled city which once had teemed with people about their business, but was now a showplace and near-empty.

They came down again to the port to dine in a restaurant called La Cave at candlelit tables under great semi-circular stone arches, feet thick, wreathed in fishermen's gear of all kinds and hung with looped seaweed trailing to the floor.

There was no lighting other than the candles, and it took them some time to accustom their eyes to the gloom. Then Bruce leaned across the table to ask, 'See anyone you know who's dining here too?'

Cleo looked around her, following the slight tilt of his head. 'Yes,' she agreed. Some distance away, at a table commanding a view of the whole floor, Luc was sitting opposite Rachel Navarre. At that moment Rachel caught Cleo's eye, raised a hand in greeting and spoke to Luc, who nodded formally, then looked away.

Bruce grinned, 'That looked as if it hurt! You'd think I was poaching the man's preserves by taking you out, the old dog in the manger. Who's the regal lass with him, do you know?' Cleo told him and his brows went up. 'His attorney, eh? Entertaining her business-wise, you think? You must be joking! I bet they're out on the town like us. What are we going to do after dinner, by the way? Are there any nightclubs to go to?'

'Several.'

'As long as we don't choose the same one they do. I've no wish to be turned into petrified stone by a glance, like whoever-it-was in the fairy tale.' Bruce paused, frowning. 'Look, you aren't worried about the chap? You aren't going to let him spoil your evening?'

With an effort Cleo braced herself. 'No, of course not,' she assured him. 'And if you want to go on somewhere, there's a disco in the town, where I should doubt very much that we'd meet them.' As they went on eating she argued mentally that she had no reason to fear Luc's disapproval. Her evenings *were* her own, and she had been frank with him that she had had men friends in England who took her out. Bruce, as one of them, had been perfectly free to look her up on holiday. And as for Bruce's suggestion that Luc was jealous of him, that was absurd—grimly absurd, but absurd.

She and Bruce were at the coffee stage when there was a movement at the other table and probably at Rachel's suggestion, Cleo thought, the other two came over. Watching her, Cleo was again struck by Rachel's poise. Bruce had chosen the right word to describe her. In the severe day clothes she affected she was almost mannish. But in evening dress she was indeed regal, with a queen's gracious manner which wasn't patronising but entirely natural to her 'rank'.

I like her, thought Cleo. *I wish I could talk to her about Luc. Ask her how long she's known him ... how well.* But of course she couldn't. Knowing nothing of her relationship with Luc,

Rachel could afford to be kind to a Girl Friday named Cleo Tyndall. But she was on Luc's side, which removed any possibility that she could ever be on Cleo's. Besides, was she—or wasn't she—the woman in Paris who had been at the other end of that telephone line?

Luc and Rachel reached their table at the same time as a guitarist in knee-breeches and vivid ruffled shirt who had appeared out of the shadows to circle the room singing Corsican songs. He bowed to Luc. '*Sgio*,' and to Rachel, '*m'dame*. Now I shall sing a love-song just for you,' he announced.

Rachel laughed. 'No, no,' she protested. 'For the young folk,' pointing to Cleo and Bruce. 'Sing your love song, a serenade, for them!'

'Even so, m'dame.' And he proceeded to sing three verses of a song of which Cleo didn't understand a word. Fortunately, she thought, while she was too acutely aware of Luc's dark gaze upon her.

Bruce thanked the man and gave him money. Luc did the same and Rachel asked for Bruce to be introduced to her. She asked him what of Corsica he had seen and planned to see and said, 'Whatever else you miss, you must see our sea caves east of the town—the grotto known as the Bath of Venus and the great cave called Sdragonatu further on. You may swim in both, but you must venture into Sdragonatu only in fair weather. Isn't that so?' she appealed to Luc.

'Unless you're an experienced boatman you don't try conclusions with either, in fair weather or foul,' he said.

'Then they'll engage an experienced man. Any fisherman on the quay would take them,' Rachel claimed, and admonished Bruce, 'Now remember—it is an adventure you must not allow Cleo to miss.' As she laid a hand on Luc's arm, saying, 'Shall we go?' she laughed, 'You could say I've banged a pretty tambourine for Corsican romance tonight. I have ordered a love-song for a pair of sweethearts, and I've sent them to bathe in our grotto of Venus. What more could my native island ask?'

Cleo and Bruce did not hear Luc's reply.

When they had gone Bruce asked, '*Is* she Corsican?'

'Yes.'

'Vidame too?'

'No, he's French.'

'And my idea that they're courting—right?'

'I—don't know. They're old friends. She came back here from Paris after he'd planned the La Réserve project.'

'It must have taken a pot of money?'

'I suppose so.' Fearing a slip of her tongue might reveal she knew more about Luc's past than was likely she would, Cleo changed the subject to relate some of the customs and taboos that were peculiarly Corsica's own. Bruce listened with interest to the incident of the *attacar* which Rachel and Luc had discussed in Cleo's hearing, but seemed to have failed to grasp its dire point.

'Mean to say that if I fancy you, I've only to kiss you in public or snitch your handkerchief or whatever—and that's a signal for all the other guys to keep off the grass? Super system, I'll say!' he marvelled.

Cleo disillusioned him. 'Not that at all. I can't have told it clearly. A man would only do that to insult some enemy of his behind the girl—her father or husband or any man who claimed a better right to her,' she corrected him.

'Then let's try it——' Half-rising, he bent across the table and kissed her. 'There! That was public enough. Or doesn't it work unless the enemy is there to witness it?'

Taken aback, she laughed shakily. 'I don't know. I think it's the publicity that counts. But what was the point? There's no enemy of yours with a prior right to *me*.'

'Ha! What about Autocrat Vidame, then?'

Slightly irritated now, 'He was only spelling out to you the conditions I'd agreed to, to get the job,' she said.

'Only pulling rank for the sake of it, huh? Well, you could have fooled me. The man had daggers in his eyes!' Bruce claimed theatrically, unabashed by her quick frown of denial.

It was not until the day before Bruce was due to leave that his booking of a man to take them out to the caves dovetailed with an unexpected free afternoon for Cleo. But when they arrived to be picked up, the quay was empty. No man was there to meet them, with or without a boat.

'It's siesta time, of course,' Cleo suggested.

'Yes, but I *arranged* with him—even drew a clock-face to make sure he understood,' Bruce protested. 'I'm going to knock somebody up. That hut down there—come with me and do the talking if we have to argue the toss as to why our guy has let us down.'

The hut was occupied by two elderly fishermen, mending nets. Yes, they knew the man Georges. Where was he? Gone this morning by mule-cart to the village of his great-aunt, to her funeral. No, no chance at all that he would be back today. He would stay for the funeral-feast and the dancing and the singing. And no, neither of the net-menders could step into the breach. Within an hour or so they had a pressing appointment with the fish in the opposite direction, and their nets were not yet ready.

Bruce fumed ineffectually. The net-mending went placidly on. Then one of the men offered, 'I have a boat with a motor for hire. You could have that.'

When Cleo interrupted this Bruce said, 'Well, that's the answer. We'll take ourselves.'

Cleo demurred, 'We were told we must have a guide.'

'In bad weather.'

'Luc Vidame said in either good or bad.'

'He was over-reacting to the idea that *I'd* be going with you. Anyway, look,' Bruce added with assumed patience, 'I may be only a sparks-boffin seamanwise, but I can handle a boat, and I'm not proposing to set out across the Atlantic in a cockleshell. Ask them how far along the coast these caves are.'

The Bath of Venus, they heard, was near the harbour mouth; they couldn't miss the large entrance to Sdragonau under the beetling limestone cliffs further on.

'Easy,' said Bruce, handling the small boat with skill in the blue calm of the harbour and using a trough of one of the rougher breakers beyond the point to slide the boat on to the lake-smooth floor of the Bath of Venus. They circled the pool, marvelling at the rippling light which flashed on to the natural carving of the roof and walls, but they decided against swimming there, and went out to follow the coastline to the larger cave.

The entrance to this was a huge archway hung with stalactites; beyond a kind of hallway a lower arch led into a great chamber floored by water, walled by jagged rock and far, far above, open to the sky. The water here flashed with ever-changing facets of colour—greens and lilacs and golds, reflections from the walls and under-water rock weeds and the glint of sunlight from overhead.

Bruce hitched the boat to a jag of rock, they got out of slacks and shirts and dived into water, smooth and warm as silk. As they dried off in the boat afterwards Bruce remarked, 'Odd, that on such a super afternoon we've had both these places to ourselves,' and in the curtained peace of their lake there was nothing to tell them why, until their glimpse of the sky seemed to darken, and there was a roar which they hadn't heard earlier from beyond the inner arch.

'Maybe we'd better go,' said Bruce, casting off and urging the engine into life. It settled to a chug-chug, the boat glided out from the inner arch, and the sinister roar was explained. Beyond the outer arch rain was falling in slanting rods, and the sea was heaving and tossing, the highest waves licking at the tips of the stalactites, the undertow sucking greedily back to feed the next onslaught on its way in.

Cleo caught her breath in sudden fear. 'Bruce, what——?'

'Could be what they warned us against—the weather changing suddenly.' He was having difficulty in steadying the boat already. 'In this, cockleshell is right. I was a fool,' he admitted grimly.

'What do we do?'

'Wait, I suppose. Wait our chance to slip out in a trough if one happens.' He reached to squeeze her hand. 'Sorry, Cleo love,' he began, then—— 'There! Missed it. I think we could have got through then. I must concentrate.'

He kept the boat rocking, shaking his head to Cleo's suggestion they should go back to the calm water they had left. 'No knowing how much water can suck right in there, and then we *should* be trapped,' he said. 'That arch is a lot too low for comfort.'

They waited. In desperation Cleo was scanning the walls of their prison in search of a ledge or a platform they could reach when there was a shout from Bruce—'Listen!' and she did—to a sound that was different from the roar of the sea. It was the mechanical beat of an engine, and in the hollow of a wave another motor-boat swept in, circled and steadied. The man at the controls was Luc.

His single word, 'Well!' addressed to Bruce, Bruce was wise enough not to attempt to answer. Luc brought his boat alongside, reached for Cleo and almost dragged her into it. To Bruce he said then, 'Get yours nose to my stern. When I open up, give her all she's got and *follow*.' A few seconds later he revved his engine into power, yelled to Cleo, 'Lie flat!', flung her face downward in the bottom of the boat when she hesitated, squatted himself at the wheel and bashed through the churning cauldron out into the open sea, Bruce's boat rocking and bucketing behind him.

He straightened and gave a hand to Cleo to help her up. She took it and sat on the cross-seat, hunched, soaked and shivering with cold. She felt too miserable and guilty to ask him how he had managed to come to their rescue, and after one glance behind to see that Bruce was following, he turned in silence in the direction of the harbour.

The man who had hired his boat to Bruce was waiting on the quay to take it over. Luc left the other one in his charge and spoke to Bruce for the first time since they had left the cave.

'How did you get down here?' he asked.

'Some people who were coming into town gave us a lift.'

'Then you'd better come back with me. My car is outside the Port Office.'

It was an uneasy journey. To Bruce's attempted thanks and explanations Luc returned a taut, 'And so the next time you try going one better than our elements, it's to be hoped it will be only your own skin that you will risk,'—a retort so ungracious as to reduce Bruce to a resentful silence and for Cleo to suffer shame on his behalf.

At his request Luc dropped him off at his tent. He said to Cleo, 'Dinner tonight?' She nodded very slightly, and Luc drove on. At her chalet he said, 'Use your key and get yourself some dry clothes. I'll wait.' When she stared, not moving, he said irritably, 'Look, every minute you sit there, my upholstery gets that much wetter. So please do as I say.'

'But why? I can go in, and naturally I shall change straight away!'

'Though I'd doubt if you have any cognac in your larder?'

'No, but——'

'Nor a bath. And as you need both and can get them at my place, that's what you'll do. Get your things.'

As she did so, Cleo wondered at herself. Even in a disgrace with him which she hadn't invited and didn't deserve, except in having indulged Bruce's eagerness to make the trip, she didn't seem able to resist Luc's autocracy. The pull of his magnetism was still too much for her. Without, now, ever yielding anything of himself in return, he could command any obedience of her, trivial or crucial, and it would be there for him. Outwardly she might rebel, defy him in words, but the truth she faced was that her essential will would always melt to his. Just as, if he should ever touch her again in love, her whole body, every sense she possessed, would reach out to answer and surrender to everything he asked, so strongly and irrevocably had their brief days of marriage bound her to him.

Nothing could have been more impersonally practical than his behaviour when they reached his villa. First he went to the bathroom and came back.

'I've put out towels and begun to run your bath,' he said. 'There's a hand-shower as well, if you want to use it.' Then he poured a strong brandy which he passed to her, standing in a damp huddle in the middle of the room.

She handed back the glass. 'It's too strong. I can't—— Some soda or water, please,' she begged.

He added a single squirt of soda and gave it back. 'If you can't drink it down, take it with you, but drink it. When you're ready, the first door on the right past the kitchen.' He looked down at his shirt and slacks, as thoroughly wet as hers. 'Could do with a change myself. But a drink is a priority with me, if not with you.'

In his bathroom a perfumed steam was rising gently from the bath. Cleo turned the water to run a little faster, then dropped her clothes and the swimsuit she had worn under them on to the floor. She tried the bathwater and was about to step in when she realised that though she had brought her dry change with her, she had left her bag in the living-room, and her comb was in it. She looked about for something more than a towel to wrap round her, and saw Luc's short bathrobe on a hook on the door. Before she had turned off the hot tap she had heard a door close, which she concluded was the one to his room, so she shouldn't have to meet him in slipping quietly out and back again.

As she had expected, the outer room was empty. She found her bag but turning, collided noisily with a chair, stumbled and fell to her knees, her open bag spilling its contents about her.

She crawled and groped for them—a mistake, for in the next instant Luc was there, in the process of putting his arms into a clean shirt and effectually barring her escape back to the bathroom.

For a long moment they both froze in tableau. Luc had made no move to fasten or to tuck in the shirt and it hung loosely from his shoulders in white contrast to the golden bronze of his chest. Cleo had knelt up, but she remained on her knees, hotly aware that her convulsive clutch at the unbelted robe had hidden her nudity from him too late. He had seen it, appraised it clinically, as having little of interest to him. From his expression Galatea, while she was still marble, could hardly have moved Pygmalion less. And now, the moment over, Luc stooped to pick up her lipstick case from the floor, handed it to her and began to button his shirt.

In another time . . . in another place they

would have laughed. She would have gone to him, or he would have come to her. They would have nuzzled like a pair of young animals; joked together in the titillating currency of lovers, and aroused by each other's nearness and desire, flesh would have spoken to flesh. In another time . . . in another place.

But not now. She stood up. He said, 'What happened?' She explained and fled, and did her best to brace herself for the post-mortem on the afternoon's happenings which he was bound to conduct.

He did. When she emerged from the bathroom he was waiting in the living-room and without preliminary accused her,

'You were there when I warned your friend Howard that in any kind of weather at all, no one should venture into Sdragonatu without a skilled guide?'

'Yes.'

'But you still abetted him in it?'

Cleo frowned. ' "Abetted" sounds criminal. I think that irresponsible was all that either of us were. And I agreed to go with him because he *had* done his best to make proper arrangements. It wasn't his fault they'd broken down, and as it was his last day here, he wouldn't have another chance. And besides——'

'Yes? "Besides"?' Luc prompted.

'Well, I do doubt whether you have the right

to censure him for something which turned out to be foolhardy in the circumstances. Me, yes; I'd disobeyed an order which I'd heard and understood. But Bruce Howard is a client of La Réserve, and he could well claim he was entitled to act on his own judgment, not yours. It was a perfect afternoon; he showed he was skilled enough to get both into and out of the caves, if the wind hadn't changed and whipped up the sea as it did, and he couldn't be expected to foresee that.'

'Famous Last Words—Nobody told me!' sneered Luc. 'But he had been told, even if I hadn't spelled out the actual shape of the danger. He must have realised there was some kind of risk. But he still chose to put your life in danger as well as his own.'

'The fisherman whose boat he had didn't warn him.'

'Can you blame the man? He had a boat for hire,' Luc pointed out dryly. 'Meanwhile, if I hadn't had business at the port and happened to hear that you had gone out, where might the two of you have been by now? Clinging to an upturned keel behind a wall of water in Sdragonatu —or worse. *That's* where!'

Cleo nodded dumbly, knowing he was right, but at a loss for words to express a gratitude which he was certain to scorn. And he went on, 'What's more, you could let your hindsight consider the effect on the reputation of La Réserve if it were supposed we'd given our blessing to a crazy enterprise which had had fatal results. Or even near-fatal. It wouldn't have made a pretty story.'

That hardened her against him. On the night she had mislaid her key he had been emphatic that he couldn't afford scandal for the estate, and it looked as if his anger now sprang as much from the same cause as from his concern for her narrow escape. She said very quietly, 'In other words, you're afraid of the headlines? Let's see —how might they go? "Guest And Woman Employee Involved In Fatal Accident" and that would hurt? You care about this place *so* much?'

She saw his dark eyes snap with anger. Then he shrugged. ' "An ill-favoured thing, but mine own",' he quoted indifferently, watched as she slung her handbag and the unsightly bundle of her dank clothes, and went to open the door for her.

(*Yes. Yours—bought with the price you got for marrying me.*) But the bitterness of that was only in her mind and went unspoken. The love she still had for him barred it from her lips.

CHAPTER FIVE

THE next morning Cleo breakfasted with Bruce in the restaurant, but she was busy with inventories when he left for the airport with a party of other people. Overnight, at dinner, he had been subdued and fully ready to blame himself for the afternoon's happenings, and more willing than was Cleo to acknowledge that Luc was justified in his anger.

'The fellow has never had any use for me,' he argued. 'In his view his contract had bought you, body and soul; I turn up, all beaming camaraderie, laying claim to at least some of your time. He sees that as cool nerve on my part and rank insubordination on yours. So perhaps there's no wonder he blows his top when he finds himself with a genuine grouse against me. Especially when, as I suspect, he has a dog-in-the-manger eye lifting your way.'

Cleo had denied indignantly, 'That's nonsense. When you arrived and I was fool enough to faint, apparently on seeing you, I think he did decide you were some skeleton I'd kept in my cupboard, after my denying I was tied by anything or anyone. But jealous? Interested in me for myself?

No! That's the very last thing——'

Bruce had shrugged. 'If you say so. But I thought I'd recognised the signs. But if it wasn't righteous malice against me and worry for you, he could still have a point. Namely, that it wouldn't have looked too good for the reputation of this place if, through my idiocy, the two of us had been lost at sea. You can imagine the kind of blow-up the locals and the papers would have made of it, not to mention any enemies he may have, and a man of his self-made tycoonery must have some.'

Cleo said sharply, 'How did you guess?'

'About his enemies?'

'No. That from what he said to me after we'd left you, I got the impression, or more than a mere impression, that his having saved the estate from gossip about its safety arrangements *was* his chief concern. Not his having been able to save us both from drowning, but the saving of La Réserve's face. How did you guess?'

To that Bruce had said, 'His obvious dedication to it, I suppose. He obviously lives for it, and you can imagine the effect of a bit of scandal or a disaster on any place that exists on its good name. Sends the public screaming in the opposite direction. I've seen it happen. Makes me feel I ought to look up the man before I leave, and creep with the contrition I really feel,' he had concluded.

But Luc was not to be found on the estate, and

Bruce's telephone call to his Bonifacio apartment went unanswered. He and Cleo sat for a long while over dinner and when he kissed her on leaving her at her chalet, he said, 'I suppose the only thing I can hope is that there are no *other* skeletons lurking in your cupboard?'

'No—living ones.'

'I thought the whole point of skeletons was that they were dead? But you mean there have been some for you?'

'One,' she admitted.

'A man?'

'Yes.'

'Existing for you before you joined the Line and I met you?'

'Yes, before that.'

'But he's not likely to rise up and claim you now? You were in love with him? Did he love you?'

'I thought so at the time, and it hurt a lot when I found he couldn't have. He wouldn't want to claim me now. It all happened an age ago, and we'll both have changed out of recognition. Meeting now, we'd be like strangers,' Cleo said.

'But there's still no serious chance for me or any of the other guys in our set?' At the reluctant shake of her head, Bruce went on, 'At the end of the season here, will you be going for this management idea, or will you come back to England?'

But she told him she couldn't answer that. It all depended—She mightn't be given the option to stay on. She might decide against taking it, if she were. She would stay as long as she could help Anne Marlowe. Meanwhile, she managed to joke, Bruce could rest assured that she wouldn't be falling for any hairy Corsican bandit.

'For which, thanks be, as much for your sake as for mine,' he applauded with a grin.

'Why for mine?'

'Obvious, I'd think. What do you suppose your life and limb would be worth at the hands of your respected Dictator if, having got rid of me, he found you going steady with one of the local lads you'd taken up with since?' Bruce quipped, and kissing her lightly again, waved, 'See you in the morning,' and had left her.

He was not serious in his courtship of her, she knew. He was still playing the field of two or three girls whom he took out, and she knew of one pretty young Dutch stewardess whose sun of happiness rose and set with him. But his pointed questions about her own future had crystallised a problem from which she had hitherto been able to shy away, since only Luc had mentioned the possibility of her being asked to stay on at the end of the season, now halfway through its course. She had heard nothing yet from either Richard or from Anne, but when they asked her

—if they did, what was she going to say? What could she bear to say?

Safety lay in No—danger in Yes. In refusing without good reason, she would sacrifice Anne's friendship and Richard's opinion of her goodwill and her ability. In accepting, she would invite her continuing humiliation at Luc's hands, and the middle way, the 'I don't know' of indecision, she despised.

But when, a few days later, Richard put the question to her it was the middle way she took. Her first reaction was to thank him eagerly— too eagerly, she realised when her later cautions, 'May I have time to think about it?' disappointed him, she could see.

He said, not distantly, but a shade more coolly, 'I'm sorry. Both Anne and I have been thinking that we had only to ask you and we'd have you in the bag, so to speak. And I hear from Luc that he suggested the possibility on your very first day.'

Cleo agreed, 'Yes, he did. Though of course without expecting me to decide then.'

'So early? Naturally not. But since then, enjoying your work and doing it as well as you do, I'd have thought you would know. However, if it's time that you want——'.

'It is, please. A little,' she pleaded. And then at a tangent asked, 'Has Luc said—— Does he think I ought to stay?'

Richard looked surprised by the question. 'But of course. I assure you, we're all of the same mind about you and of your value to us. So don't take too long about your decision, will you?'

Still without knowing what she would make it, merely putting off the evil hour, she promised that she would not, and he went on more cordially, 'I'm taking Anne into the local hospital this afternoon for a few days' observation. Her confinement will be in Ajaccio, but they can do her tests here. So if you have to be in the town tomorrow, or you have a free hour, pop in and see her, will you? I'll tell her you will try to come.'

Another visitor, Rachel Navarre, was with Anne when Cleo arrived. Neither of them had long with her, as she was called to her appointment very soon. The other two left the hospital together, and Cleo, who had driven down, offered a lift to Rachel who was walking.

Rachel thanked her but declined. 'I have to see a client who lives quite near, and as I allowed myself more time than I got with Anne, I'm too early. So why don't we have coffee or an ice together, if you haven't to go straight back?' she suggested.

Though she didn't know what use, if any, she could make of it, it was an opportunity Cleo remembered wanting on the night Rachel and Luc had dined at La Cave. Rachel was friendly, approachable, and whatever she was to Luc, she was a link with those hidden five years. Luc liked her, trusted her, if no more than that. So how much might he have confided in her? Cleo wondered, and though knowing she dared not ask, hoped that indirectly she might learn from Rachel.

They ordered ices at an open-air café, and before their waiter came back, Rachel put an abrupt question. 'Anne tells me you couldn't give Richard a direct answer when he invited you to stay on at La Réserve at the end of the season. Why not?' she demanded.

This was sooner than Cleo had reckoned on having to justify her indecision. 'I—well, I only said I needed a little time to think about it,' she evaded.

'You have another job to go to? Or one in view?' Rachel pressed.

'No, nothing. Unless I went back to the one I left.'

'But you have been happy here? Settled down? Enjoyed your work?' Rachel paused. 'Or aren't you able to let all that count against some personal clash you find too much for you? Could be something like that, perhaps?' At Cleo's involuntary start, she added, 'Yes?' and when Cleo did not answer she smiled.

'Come,' she said gently, 'if that's your problem, you can tell me, for I'm a kind of Elder Statesman to La Réserve and I'm used to untangling all

sorts of knots for it. And as I can't believe you
are at odds with either Richard or Anne, could it,
by any chance, be Luc?'

If she said Yes, Rachel would expect her to
elaborate. So Cleo said No, and though she
thought Rachel's brows drew together in faint
disbelief, she burned her boats by adding quickly,
'It was just that I wasn't quite prepared for
Richard's asking me to stay. But I do want to. I
would like to, if they—all—want me to.'

Rachel nodded her satisfaction. 'They do, I assure you. You would hardly credit the little fly-
by-nights they endured before you came—one a
local girl, two from the French mainland, and all
of them seeing the job as their password to the
favour of some rich bachelor tourist, complete
with yacht. Which was why, though I told him
he had no right to ask it, Luc insisted on that
arrogant clause in their advertisement for An
English girl. But it didn't worry you?'

Cleo shook her head. 'No. I had no commitments in England.' Then she couldn't resist adding a question which should not be too dangerous. 'Have you acted for La Réserve ever since
Luc Vidame started it?' she asked.

'Not "ever since". He already had the project
off the ground by nearly two years when I came
back here from Paris,' said Rachel.

'You had known each other in Paris?' Cleo
wanted it confirmed.

'Oh yes. And long before that too.'

Cleo swallowed hard. 'Long before?'

'Years. My return here was a second reunion for us; a picking up of threads. Hasn't he ever mentioned how we used to play together here on the island?'

'You played as children?'

'Not as children. We were teenagers—fifteen, sixteen or so. And not here. On the beach at Calvi in the north, where his mother had cousins and where he used to come for his summer holidays.'

(Teenagers? Almost ready for romance and to meet later?) Embroiled now, Cleo asked recklessly, 'And then you met again in Paris?'

'While I was at law school and for a time after I qualified. For a Corsican girl, I was one of the lucky ones, as my parents were modern enough to want me to have a career. Most daughters are expected to stay at home until they marry or have a marriage arranged for them, though I do know of one gifted youngster who escaped the net successfully. But that's another story—— Yes, Luc and I were meeting quite often, though he wasn't a fixture. He had enough money to live on, but hadn't decided on a career. He used to go down to the Riviera, and he came back here once or twice, I know. As I did myself on vacation, but not at the same time, and when I did come back for good, as I told you, he had La Réserve well under way. And that without any capital to speak of.'

Cleo drew a sharp breath. 'He had no capital? Surely——?'

'He says not. He had the ideas and the foresight. The authorities saw the need for some development of this coast. There were wealthy gnomes with the money to lend for it, and after a lot of sweet-talking by Luc, he was given the word to go ahead. And now, except for the current loan on the new marina bay, the estate is pretty well solvent.'

Puzzled, her mind full of questions she must not ask, Cleo said, 'That's an achievement. It shows what one man can do.'

Rachel agreed, 'Yes indeed. But Luc has changed a lot in the doing.'

'Changed?' (So—not only to me? thought Cleo.)

Rachel nodded. 'From the playboy he used to be. He has hardened; tends to expect too much, and though he sees to it that he usually gets what he demands, sometimes it has been at the price of a friendship and a regard he needs. That's why it's good that he has Anne and Richard and you, one hopes, so loyally behind him——'

'You too,' said Cleo.

'I? Oh, I've always been there,' Rachel laughed. She looked at her watch and rose. 'I've been gossiping too long. I must go,' she said, and Cleo went with her, glad she couldn't know that her willing talk about Luc had been to a wife who should have known him better than anyone, and did not.

When she was alone the tape of Cleo's memory reeled back for her what she had learned.

As she had guessed, Rachel and Luc were much of an age. They had played—flirted?—together in their teens. And later? For years they had both been in Paris, or leaving it and coming back to it from time to time, and they probably telephoned each other when they did.

Rachel knew of Luc's regular jaunts to the Riviera, but either she knew nothing of his marriage or she was not revealing that part of his story. But—on that afternoon in Menton, the woman on the other end of the telephone line *had* known of it! Cleo never failed to cringe inwardly at the memory of hearing herself described as 'an immature green apple' only too ready to fall to Luc's charms. So had that woman been Rachel Navarre—or hadn't she? And if she were not— and, liking Rachel, Cleo hoped not—who, then, was that other shadowy figure in Luc's past? Had Luc kept her as secret from Rachel as he had kept the fact of his marriage from her—if indeed she did not know of it?

After all, he had deceived her with one glaring lie. He had allowed her to believe that he had financed the birth of La Réserve with other people's money and confidence, not his own. But he had had money! He had bought his inheritance with a loveless marriage of convenience, and would probably have played the part of ardent bridegroom for as long as it suited him, if the girl who had 'made a willing gift of herself' hadn't found him out. Cleo felt angry and sick that she should still cling to the memory of his wooing of her and his skilled lovemaking which had enslaved her need of him to the point where she still could not break free of the dream that it had all been as real for him as for her; the dream that passion would surge again between them, that love would mean what it said. For now he was a living contradiction of the man she had married in such faith. Even Rachel Navarre knew it of him, and she hadn't suffered at his hands as Cleo had. He respected Rachel, even if he did not love her. For Cleo he had nothing but contempt.

The next event on La Réserve's calendar was the opening of the new mooring-bay—another tribute to Luc's uncanny capacity for getting things done ahead of schedule. Anne Marlowe duly cut a ribbon and broke a bottle of champagne in the right place, and in the evening the estate gave a dinner and dance in Bonifacio's principal hotel.

Anne and Richard were going in their own car. Anne told Cleo, 'Luc will call for you, and you'll be sitting with us at the top table, along with the local V.I.P.s and Luc's architect.'

Except for her dinner with Bruce, it was Cleo's first evening function. She had a choice of two or three dresses which no one had seen, and she was tempted to wear the newest and most expensive of them. But its line was daring, its corsage-plunge too revealing, and what was she, she reminded herself bitterly, but one of Luc's 'hired help'? The others? In one, a boldly flowered organza with a skirt which whispered and floated, she always felt comfortable and free. But could she? Dared she? she wondered, as she shook out a third and held it against herself before her mirror.

It was black, ankle-length and of sheathlike fitting to the line of her breasts. A procession of tiny silver buttons marched from its centre-hem to the point of cleavage, where it divided to scroll a spiderweb of silver on the swell of each breast. The cowl neckline draped close to the base of her throat. The sleeves were long and tight to the braceleting of three rows of silver buttons at the wrist.

Black though it was, it was by no means the season-in, season-out 'little black dress' of dowdy use. It was incredibly slimming and, demure as its effect was, it was studiedly so. She could still wear it; her figure had not altered in the five years that she had kept it by her—for memory's sake. When she had worn it for Luc, he had called her his black pencil with a silver point.

'Meaning my buttons?' she had queried.

'And your hair,' he had said, lifting it with a finger to kiss the nape of her neck.

And so—supposing she wore it, would he notice it? Would any man remember a dress from so long ago?

When he came for her she was ready except for her wrap. She watched him appraise her, his eyes travelling over her from her head to her feet. He held her wrap for her to put on, and he might have been draping a sheet over a shop-window dummy. When they went out he locked the door for her and dropped the key into his pocket.

She held out her hand for it. 'You've kept my key.'

'You won't need it. I shall be seeing you home,' he said.

At the dinner table she was several places away from him, his partner the wife of the Mayor of Bonifacio, with Anne on his other side. Cleo never learned the function in civil life of her own partner, his French being so Corsican-accented that she understood little that he said. On her right was Rachel's partner, Luc's architect, who spoke good English, and she talked with them most of the time.

Afterwards Anne made several introductions for her and she found herself in demand for dancing. When she was not dancing she was able to watch Luc moving among his guests, without anyone's knowing that he was the one man in the room for her, the only one. She was sitting talking to Anne when he appeared at her side. 'Will you dance?' he said, and held out his hand.

His inviting her was all part of their public image, she told herself, but she was trembling a little as she went into his arms for the waltz. They had always fitted so well . . . slim legs following the lead of muscular hard ones, hips close, body to body, his breath just wafting her hair, and when she looked up, their secret little smile for each other. And even now, nobody watching would have guessed that it was only expertise which made them appear to be one entity as they danced, that Luc was only doing his social duty to her, that there was no fussing, no interlocking, no sharing between them, except for the duration of the dance.

Later, her last partner had left her and she was sitting alone when a girl she had noticed several times crossed the floor towards her, walked past, hesitated, then came back.

She was petite, with very dark eyes, and wore her hair swept into an extravagant bunch at one side of her head. Her red dress and a single hooped earring accentuated her gipsy looks.

She said, '*Vous parlez français, madame?*'

Cleo smiled. '*Un petit peu, madame.*'

'Ah—then I may——?' Taking Cleo's permission for granted, she sat down beside her. 'I may perhaps ask a kindness of you—nothing much?'

'Anything I can do,' Cleo told her cordially.

'Well, it is like this,' the girl confided. 'I am a stranger in Bonifacio; I come from Calvi. At the moment I am staying at a small hotel near by. I was invited to this Dinner through a friend who wasn't sure whether he could come himself or not, and indeed he hasn't come. But he suggested that I come alone—which I did, and now I am wondering whether you would introduce me to our host, whom I've never met—just to excuse my friend's absence to him, and to thank him for my own evening. You would do that for me?'

Surprised by the request, but supposing that the girl had only been invited as 'and friend' to Luc's invitee, Cleo said, 'Of course, if we can catch him alone. He is rather in demand.'

The girl nodded. 'So I see. And I hadn't quite the courage to march up to him, hold out my hand and say "I am Rosel Rostand. How do you do, monsieur?"' She looked about her. 'There are others who have been with him more than you have—but, for example, the tall goddess he has been escorting most looked too aloof to ask—and so I asked you, who looked kind—as you have proved.'

Cleo said, 'The tall woman is Mademoiselle Navarre, Monsieur Vidame's lawyer; she wouldn't have snubbed you, I am sure.' Though Cleo her-

self was rather diffident about making the introduction, she had promised, so as soon as she saw
Luc was standing alone, she told the girl, 'Come
now. Your name—Rostand, did you say?
Mademoiselle Rostand? Or Madame?'

'Mademoiselle, please.'

When Cleo made the introduction she saw
Luc's eyes flash with interest at Rosel Rostand's
exotic looks. She left them talking together and
went to relate the incident to Anne and Richard,
indicating the girl, who was now dancing with
Luc.

Richard shook his head. 'Don't know her from
Adam.'

'You wouldn't. She's not local. She comes from
Calvi,' Cleo pointed out.

'Did she tell you the name of the chap who
should have brought her and didn't?'

'No. Only her own.'

'Evidently got tired of being a wallflower and
decided to make for the big time with her host
for starters,' Richard commented without much
interest. But Cleo's imagination had gone to work
on the coincidence of 'Calvi'. Rosel Rostand came
from the island's northern resort; Luc had spent
his summers there as a young man and had been
back since, according to Rachel. And that day on
the telephone he had been welcoming someone's
arrival in, or return to Paris, promising they
would meet there. So was it possible——?

But this girl, appearing no older than Cleo herself, would have been only a child in Luc's late teens, and Cleo was prepared to swear she had introduced two strangers to each other just now. No, she shook off the thought. But what was this long nag of suspicion of Luc *doing* to her? she wondered. Would she ever be free of it? Only through his pity for her doubts, and that, he had made it very plain, she was not likely to get.

The evening broke up soon after midnight. In the car on the way back Cleo was just about to explain how she came to bring Rosel Rostand to him when Luc asked her just that question.

'She had seen me with you, and thought she might ask me to introduce you,' Cleo explained.

'She told you why?'

'She said she wanted to explain why her escort hadn't come, and to thank you for herself.'

'She needn't have bothered. The man's name was only given to me as a duty guest who ought to be invited,' Luc said indifferently.

'She—Mademoiselle Rostand—doesn't live around here. She's from Calvi, she said,' Cleo ventured.

'Yes.' Luc's flat monosyllable dismissed Rosel Rostand and her origins as a subject for discussion. Cleo watched her own misgivings about the girl finally vanish.

At her chalet he used her key on the door, stood aside for her to enter and followed her in.

Nervous, as wary of him as of a stranger who had forced himself upon her, Cleo gave him a stiff 'Thank you' and took off her wrap.

He did not move and once again she had an impression of tableau—two separate, still, but aware figures—she alight with longing, he ready with a weapon against her pride or her conscience or both? They had done their public duty by their onlookers, and now was he feeling he could wield the lash?

She waited. When Luc spoke it was with a seeming irrelevance which took her aback. 'Don't we pay you enough?' he asked.

She felt her expression go blank. 'Pay me? Enough? What do you mean?'

'*That.*' His contemptuous gesture was for her dress, and instinctively both her hands went to cross on her breast and throat, as if to guard the innocent offence of the dress from him. She opened her lips to speak, but he was repeating savagely, 'Well, *don't* we pay you enough, that you have to resurrect a seasons old model that one would expect should have gone to the ragbag years ago?'

So he had remembered it! Her wearing it had roused something in him, if only his anger. She drew herself up, smoothing the dress over her hips. 'It may be old, but I kept it because I've always liked it,' she said. 'I wore it tonight because it was more suitable for a dinner-party than anything else I have.'

He uttered a coarse laugh. 'The handy excuse you prepared, in case I remembered it and remarked on it?'

'I didn't think you would notice it. Men don't——'

—'And the even handier lie! You thought of everything, didn't you—hoping to be believed! Perish the thought you used it as a slimy little jog of my memory of having once admired the taste which chose it and wore it to devastating effect! It was even further from your devious plans, *of course*, that I might see it as an invitation and act accordingly? Playing with fire rather dangerously, weren't you?' he taunted her. 'I could yet be tempted!'

Cleo shrank back. Her lips barely forming the words, she said, 'To—to make love to me against my will? Or for revenge? You—wouldn't want to, and you wouldn't dare!'

He laughed again without amusement. He said, 'You mistake me. I merely meant that I could be tempted to rip the pseudo-demure thing off you— physically, with my bare hands.'

She shrank even further into herself. But she defied him, 'You wouldn't dare do that either.'

He shook his head. 'Don't be too sure.' With one swift movement he was behind her, the back of the neck of the dress in his grasp, making her skin crawl with mingled dread and delight at the touch of his hand. 'In fact,' he went on, using the material as a lever to give her a little shake, 'I could do it now with some satisfaction, if I didn't suspect you'd derive some masochistic pleasure out of trying to stop me. You'd enjoy a fight, h'm?'

When she did not reply, being almost choked by the drag of the material against the front of her throat, he administered another threatening shake and let her go.

He went to the door, making an ostentatious gesture of dusting off his hands. 'At least I think we've disposed of the excuses and the lies about your not having had discomfiture for me in view. But they never held much water, did they? What a pity you gave time to thinking them up!' he said over his shoulder as he went out.

CHAPTER SIX

CLEO told herself she had had to lie in self-defence against Luc's overweening anger. If she had admitted she had worn the dress in the hope of touching some chord of gentle memory in him, he might have humiliated her even further. But she realised too late that she shouldn't have hoped he would believe her. If he remembered the dress at all, he would have guessed it had had a purpose—and she had asked for her own punishment by daring him against the one action she feared more than the one he said he intended and almost took.

For the dress to have been stripped from her would have been bad enough. To be forced by Luc ... *no!* Her very nerves seemed to freeze at the thought. It would be a negation of all the delight she had ever known in his lovemaking, and she had to cling to her memory of that, however little it might have meant to him. She wasn't to be 'taken' at the whim of his will to dominate; her response must be her gift for the giving, or it wouldn't be there at all. (Though if he hated and despised her now, would he care?)

She had unfastened and stepped out of the

dress with one thought in mind—to destroy it.
But how? She could put it in a weighted bag and
throw it into the sea. But such an errand to the
beach seemed ludicrous. She could cut it up and
put it piecemeal in an ashcan. The idea revolted.
She could burn it—if there weren't strict rules
against fire risk on the estate. In the end she made
a slim roll of it and hid it at the back of a drawer-
ful of warmer clothes she hadn't worn since leaving England. She hoped to be able to forget it was
there.

She had grasped the nettle of her promise to
Rachel, only to find that Rachel had already told
Richard of her decision to stay on. He had congratulated her and Anne had thanked her.
Richard explained how much administration and
reorganisation had to be done in the winter, making the coming busyness, when all but the perma-
nent residents had left, sound different but excit-
ing. But for the shadow of Luc, who hadn't
commented in her hearing, she would have been
happy in the prospect before her.

Early on she had been agreeably surprised to
hear from Anne that one of the chores she
thought was among her overtime duties was that
of babysitting.

'Why, no,' Anne had assured her. 'You take it
on or not as you please, at so much an hour, and
whatever you're paid is your perk. Naturally
we're pleased if you'll do it for guests, but you

don't have to. It's for you to choose, and naturally, if it's late-night sitting, you'll expect your clients to see you home.'

But for the engagement which Cleo had about a fortnight later, she decided to use her Yellow Peril. Her clients' villa, on the outskirts of the estate, was a full kilometre from her chalet. But she knew the people; the children's father had a reputation for drinking more than he should when he had to drive; his wife did not drive. And Cleo, who had no fear of the dark, calculated that she would prefer to find her way home on her own machine than be at the doubtful mercies of Mr Godfree's escorting after a convivial evening on the town.

She parked the Yellow Peril outside the villa. Her clients swept off to their date in Bonifacio, promising to be back around eleven o'clock. The children, Emma, nine and Kate, seven, fell with welcoming whoops upon Cleo. Supper and bedtime were as yet an hour off, and there was a choice of Scrabble or Mastermind to play.

When they had gone to bed, Cleo watched television for a while, then settled down to read the book she had brought with her. She had not expected the Godfrees to keep too strictly to their promise, but when it was nearly midnight and they had not returned she began to be anxious. She looked in at the children who were fast asleep, then returned to her book and tried to concentrate on it, though straining her ears for the sound of an approaching car. She began to hatch a sense of grievance. People had no right to put other people to such anxiety, nor to keep them up and out so late! By the time one o'clock struck and a few minutes later the car drove up, she doubted her ability to be more than strictly civil with the latecomers, however 'happy' they might be.

She was ready with her report that everything had gone well with the children's evening. Then she meant to slip away. But to her dismay only Mr Godfree appeared at the door of the living-room, to lean against the lintel with a foolish leer on his face. Then he came on into the room, noisily colliding with a chair before finding its seat and flopping into it.

Automatically Cleo shushed him. 'You'll wake Emma and Kate! Where's Mrs Godfree?' she asked.

'Lynda?' He pondered the name. 'Oh—left her behind. Wouldn't come with me, so left her t'get home by herself. *When* she's good and ready.'

'But she hasn't a car. She can't drive!' Cleo protested.

'Someone'll bring her. Plenty of our pals at the party glad to——' He looked about him. 'Say we have a drink, you and I? Just a little nightcap— yes?'

'No,' snapped Cleo. 'I must go, and you should go to bed.'

'Must wait for Lynda. Have a drink meanwhile. You too.' He made a lunge towards a cupboard, throwing its doors wide with a crash which made Cleo wince and hesitate as to what she ought to do. At this volume of clumsy noise he could well wake the children and frighten them, and even if they had the courage to investigate, he was in no fit state to put them at their ease. Perhaps she ought to wait with him for a while, for surely, unless his wife was as irresponsible as he, she couldn't delay too long in getting herself a lift and coming home?

So she said, 'Very well. I'll wait with you for Mrs Godfree for a little while.' She nodded towards one of the two glasses he held. 'Just a ginger ale, if you have one, please.'

He poured cognac into his own glass and set it down. 'Ginger ale—*and* something in it,' he said of the other glass. 'Gin? Vodka? What's your poison?'

'Ginger ale—neat,' she insisted, and moved towards him, prepared to pour it herself if necessary. But before she reached him he had poured a little something—she couldn't see what—and held it high out of her reach as he caught her round her waist with his other hand, holding her captive while he laughed tipsily.

'Forfeit!' he crowed. 'A nice friendly kiss—or

two—or three, if we like each other. And then ginger ale it shall be—cross my heart.'

'Let me *go*!' Cleo struggled and plucked at his fingers, to no avail.

'Come *on*,' he urged. 'Sporty, attractive girl like you, I bet you aren't too fussy about where your kisses go. So what about it? Who's going to tell?'

But as she shrank from the pulpy lips which sought her mouth but only caught her swiftly turned cheek, she saw that someone was standing at the open door behind him; someone who had walked into the house unheard; not Mrs Godfree, but Luc. He just stood there, looking on.

Cleo went limp within the drunken man's hold. 'Give in, huh? Well now, don't you all, sooner or later?' he chuckled, and lowered the hand holding the glass, setting it down beside his own. He turned, saw Luc and nodded amiably. 'Tha's right, walk straight in, chum. Don't bother to knock. Lady and I just having spot of indoor games and a drink.' He tapped one glass. 'Mine— a cognac.' He tapped the other. 'Lady's fancy— neat vodka. What'll I make y——?'

Luc cut in, 'All right. Joke over.' He nodded curtly to Cleo. 'Go and get in my car, I'm driving you home.'

She did not obey. 'You don't understand. Mrs Godfree isn't home yet——'

'That's evident.'

'But I oughtn't to leave until—— The children——'

'Are still asleep—or not, as may be. *Go and get
in the car!*'

This time she went, a lump of indignation at
his misjudgment of the scene almost physically
choking her. She stood waiting by his car when
he joined her a few minutes later. She said, 'I
came on my moped. I'll have to take it back.'

Luc said, 'Leave it. It can be fetched in the
morning. Seeing it outside was my clue to your
being here—a lot too late.' He opened the car
door for her and she got in. 'You were—allegedly
—baby-sitting, I gather?'

'Baby-sitting,' she said firmly. 'Not allegedly.
Actually.'

'Until this hour? You had no right to agree to
stay so late.'

'I didn't. Until eleven, they said. But they
hadn't come by one o'clock, and then it was only
Mr Godfree who came alone.'

'Whereupon, with one of them returned, you
were free to leave him to it, and come away.'

'I wanted to. I nearly did. And now you *have*,'
she accused.

'Only while I see you safe. I'm going back, and
if I have to put him to bed with his boots on,
that's where he's going.'

'Yes, well——" Cleo went on, 'he was drunk
and being so noisy that he was bound to wake the

children. So I agreed to stay until Mrs Godfree did turn up. It seems she'd refused to go with him, and she was relying on a lift to bring her when she did come.'

'And meanwhile you were making a party of it—kiss-in-the-ring games and all?'

'I was making the best of it. He made me say what I would drink, and I told him ginger ale.'

'Ginger ale? That was vodka in your glass. They aren't even the same colour!'

'I didn't see what he'd put in the glass, and I hadn't touched it when he taunted me by holding it away from me until——' She paused, biting her lip. 'And you—you saw the rest.'

'I saw enough to justify my coming in uninvited when nobody answered my knock. I thought, when I warned you, that you claimed you were proof against maudlin drunks on the prowl for easy conquest?'

'And so I am.'

'Yet you hadn't enough caution to keep distance between you. How do I know you weren't enjoying the silly skirmish as much as he seemed to be?'

They had reached her chalet and she let him cut the car engine before she spoke. Then she said in a low intense voice, 'You know, I hope, because I'm telling you, and I'm not in the habit of lying in self-defence. I'd thought I was right to stay with that man until his wife came home; he caught me unawares and he kissed me against my will, and I wasn't playing nor enjoying any part of it. But if you don't believe me, then I've no more to say.'

She had turned towards him, and for a long moment they looked at each other across the darkness. Then Luc said, 'Very well, I believe you.'

'Thank you.' (A grudging, 'I believe you', wrung from him—was that all he had for her comfort?)

He went on, 'Though it all goes to show, doesn't it, that you aren't quite as handy with the frozen mitt as you thought?'

'Evidently not,' she agreed reluctantly.

'Then don't run foolish risks in fture. Don't lay yourself open to the idea that you're easy game. That kind of news gets around too fast.'

Cleo felt for the door-catch, and he leaned across to open it for her. 'Not of me,' she said with quiet dignity, and got out.

He didn't follow her. 'I'm glad of that,' he said, as if he meant it, and for a long while after he had left her the sincerity lit a little torch of hope within her.

If he cared that she shouldn't make herself cheap, then to that extent at least, she still mattered to him. The thought lasted as a heart-warming flame, until it occurred to her that he could be as concerned for the possibility of scandal as he was for her reputation. The torch flickered and died out.

Her moped came back early the next morning, ridden by one of the estate lads, and except that Emma and Kate Godfree romped happily over to bid her goodbye she saw no more of the family before they left the following week. The work went on. She clerked and chauffeured and interpreted and advised. She booked guided tours, played beach-guard to tinies, ironed out complaints and found herself sitting in as a trusted colleague of Anne's and Richard's ways-and-means sessions. She could have been blissfully happy, if only——

She returned from a trip to the airport one afternoon to hear Anne announce, 'I have news for you. A girl-friend of yours booked into Belafonte.'

Belafonte was the name of the next nearest chalet to Cleo's. 'A girl friend of mine?' she frowned. 'Couldn't be!'

'Could, though. Or so she says. Remember the girl you pointed out to us at the marina Dinner? Wanted an introduction to Luc, you told us. Remember her now?' asked Anne.

'Oh—yes,' said Cleo. 'What was her name? Rostand—Rosel Rostand. But she was only staying in Bonifacio, I thought?'

'Well, now she wants to stay here. Didn't want to give a definite time, but as we're well

over the peak, I accepted that, as we had Belafonte empty. She asked about you—said how
kind you'd been and seemed tickled pink to hear
she was near you.'

'Oh dear, she'll be "dropping in", I suppose,'
said Cleo.

'I shouldn't wonder,' confirmed Anne. 'She
seems the mixing sort. But if she starts being a
nuisance you can always plead a pressing date
with, say, a laundry-count or the water-meter
reader. Or—the thought strikes me—she may be
looking up Luc too. Who knows?'

That Rosel Rostand was interested in Luc was
evident from her first visit to Cleo's chalet that
evening. She brought up his name casually, but
then she wanted to know how often he was to
be seen about the estate. Did he regard his apartment in the town or his villa as his main base?
Did he mix socially with the villa residents? He
had made an outstanding success of La Réserve in
a very short time, hadn't he? Was well on the
way to becoming one of the V.I.P.s of the region?
Or so Rosel had heard. Had Cleo?

Cleo answered guardedly, puzzled by this interest in Luc's public image, until it occurred to
her that if Rosel wanted to gain Luc's favour, she
might be snob enough for it to matter to her that
he had a status she could boast about to her
friends. But what headway was she likely to make
with Luc's apparent detachment from romantic

liaisons? Cleo wondered. The girl was very attractive in a flamboyant way, and Luc had shown interest in her at the Dinner, only to dismiss her later. Had that indifference been assumed, Cleo's jealousy wanted to know. Was she going to have to stand by and watch Rosel play for and bedazzle Luc?

About herself, Rosel was not generous with information. She had been ill—no details—and was on extended leave from her job as receptionist to a fashionable Calvi doctor—not named. Cleo did not learn where or with whom, if anyone, she lived in Calvi, nor why she had chosen to come alone, first to Bonifacio and then to La Réserve for her recuperation. She had said she was single, but she mentioned no family. She said nothing more to Cleo about the man-friend who should have escorted her to the marina Dinner, and she seemed to depend for companionship on such time as Cleo could spare her and on the acquaintanceships she struck up at the bar or the pool or on the beach.

She was gay and popular, and she chose clothes in flaming jewel colours which enhanced her gipsy looks. She drove a hired sports car with flair and as soon as she had gathered a few special cronies, she gave an evening drinks party to which she invited both Cleo and Luc.

She had not often met Luc before that, Cleo thought, deploring Rosel's ploy as a childish,

awed deference towards him. She had learned
that he was known as the Big Man and called
him that, telling him she was secretly afraid of
him.

'Though if I got to know you better, I might
find you quite human—who can tell?' she invited.

Luc shrugged. 'It depends on what you mean
by human,' he said.

With her glass just at her lips and looking up
at him from under her lashes, 'Oh, come now, Big
Man,' she crooned. 'You know very well what I
mean! But if you really don't, then that's an open
challenge to any girl of spirit to teach you.'

His look at her was coolly provocative. 'Are
you applying for the job?' he asked.

She pretended to shrink from him. 'Me? I
wouldn't dare!' she declared in mock horror at
the suggestion, without deceiving Cleo at all, that
she had intended the banter as anything other
than the first round of a flirtation with Luc.

Others followed. Rosel, Cleo came to realise
jealously, had all the arts of the practised
coquette at her fingertips. She could work at and
engineer a meeting with Luc and still affect a
dimpling, coy surprise that it had happened by
the merest chance. To his face and in Cleo's hearing, she still pretended an awe of him which kept
him at arm's length, but her pursuit of him was
so purposeful and concentrated that Cleo some-

times wondered bitterly whether she had set herself a deadline for his conquest and was afraid of not making it.

For Cleo there was the slight comfort that, in public at least, Luc showed few signs of subjection to Rosel's campaign. He was as urbane and detached in her company as in Cleo's or Anne's, and as far as Cleo knew, he made no move of his own to invite it, until she heard from Anne that he and Rosel had dined together more than once in the town.

No less interested than Cleo, though for less poignant reasons, Anne announced, 'He hasn't talked to Richard, so it's anyone's guess as to how far he's hooked—if at all. But if she's worn him down to the point of some tête-à-tête dates, someone should really take her aside and warn her quietly that in our experience Luc doesn't go in at the deep end for women, and she could be wasting her time. Couldn't *you*?' Anne appealed.

'Couldn't I what?' asked Cleo.

'Put it tactfully to Rosel that if she wants Luc, her technique is all wrong. He's never let himself be chased yet. In any affair, it's always he who makes the running, and when he calls a halt, that's that.'

Turning a new knife in her wound, Cleo said carefully, 'You've known him have some affairs, then?'

'One or two, none of them serious on his side.

Which is why it might be a charity to head off young Rosel Rostand in good time. She's had her fun, got further with him than the other current lovelies round the pool, but if she isn't to get hurt, she'd be wise to call it a day now, and a hint to that effect wouldn't do any harm.'

Cleo shook her head. 'Well, I couldn't administer it, or even show her I realised how she's throwing herself at Luc. I don't know her nearly well enough. She doesn't honour me with a progress report about him, and she could be fully justified in telling me just where I get off.'

'I thought you said she'd catechised you from A to Z when she first came?' Anne objected.

'Then, yes, and I told her all I knew. But she hasn't discussed Luc since with me, and I don't suppose she wants to.'

There, however, Cleo was to be proved wrong, when Rosel began to make a point of recounting with relish her day-to-day encounters and successes with Luc. In the telling she affected a naïve surprise that he should be so taken with her ('little me!'). But neither the naïveté nor the surprise were genuine, Cleo knew. Rosel was revelling in her triumph; she needed to impress someone with it, and she forced upon Cleo the role of a convenient listening ear. It was plain that, if Rosel were telling the truth, the affair had gone far beyond the possibility of warning her that it couldn't succeed. According to her, it *was* succeeding, the proof being in the number of evenings Luc had taken her out; the carte-blanche she claimed she had for ringing him any time at his apartment, and the fact that she was always welcome to drop in at his villa for a pre-dinner drink.

Often Cleo was tempted to an explosive, 'Look, I can't stand this. Luc Vidame is mine—or I thought he was once. Until he gets rid of me, you can't have him, so if you must boast about how he's fallen for you, go and do it to somebody else.' But obviously that wasn't possible. She could only snub Rosel with a feigned lack of interest which the other girl would nudge with a plaintive 'You are not listening,' and jerk Cleo's attention back to herself.

Luc and Rosel. Luc and the unknown girl at the other end of a telephone line five years ago. Luc and his coldblooded affairs at which Anne had hinted. Cleo did not know which hurt most, though of the latter she realised she was a fool if she deluded herself that he had led a celibate existence through those five years. There must have been women for him, apart from his closeness with Rachel Navarre, and compared with those shadowy, now discarded figures, only Rachel was real and enduring and far more worthy of him than was Rosel. It wasn't easy to be jealous of Rachel. It was only too easy to burn with it over Rosel.

There came an evening when she had not seen
Rosel all day, and by the time she was thinking of
preparing for bed, she concluded thankfully that
she was to be spared the girl's irksome company
now. But she had got no further than tidying her
living-room and drawing curtains when there was
Rosel's familiar little tap on the door.

'Oh *no*!' breathed Cleo, rehearsing a short dismissal. But as soon as she opened to her, Rosel
stepped in with a bright, 'Do you mind? I'm
rather early, so may I put in some time with
you?'

Cleo closed the door slowly. 'Early?' she
echoed, glancing at her watch. 'It's a quarter to
eleven. Early for what?'

'For my date with Luc.' Rosel looked about her
and sat down. 'Have you anything to drink? I
need one.'

'Only the rest of the half-bottle of wine I had
with my supper,' Cleo told her. She had spirits
as well, but something about the glitter in the
girl's eyes and her over-confident manner told
Cleo that she seemed to be well stimulated
enough already.

'Well, that will have to do.' As Cleo poured,
'You'll join me?' Rosel asked.

'No. I told you—I had a glass with my meal.'
Cleo studied Rosel's heightened colour, her sheath
of an evening gown in green and silver lurex and
the length of slim leg revealed by its almost knee-

high split skirt. Odd, she reflected, that at this
time of night Rosel seemed to have brought no
wrap.

'You're going out somewhere with Luc?' she
asked.

Rosel giggled, choked on her sip of wine, and
giggled again. 'Not *out*,' she said with emphasis.

'I thought you said——?'

'That I had a date with him, yes. At his villa.'

Cleo felt her spine chill. 'He's invited you
there? At this time of night? Alone?'

Rosel said, 'He hasn't actually invited me. I'm
going on a date I've made for myself. Alone, and
at this time of night—or not quite yet. The timing happens to be rather important.'

'Luc doesn't know you're going to the villa,
but you expect him to welcome you when you
get there?' Cleo questioned coldly.

'Oh, he'll welcome me all right. I shall get in
and stay for as long as I need. I haven't worked
on him all this time to allow him to turn me
down tonight, just when we've got to the pay-
off.' Rosel stirred in her chair and twirled the
stem of her empty glass. She giggled again. 'I
don't deny I need a bit of Dutch courage. I do
wish you had something else to drink. Are you
sure you haven't the merest *drop* of vodka or of
cognac?'

'I haven't anything for *you* to drink,' Cleo
qualified the small lie. 'If you ask me, you've

been stoking up on courage already. Courage for what, I don't know, and I don't want to know.' Suddenly Cleo's temper flared. 'What's more, however sure you are of a welcome from Luc Vidame, you're not particularly welcome to use me as a kind of staging-post on your way to whatever climax you plan to achieve with him tonight. And this is something I ought to have made clear from the first—your successes and failures with him have nothing to do with me—nothing at all. So I'm going to bed, and you can leave as soon as you like. In fact, the sooner the better, for me.'

But Rosel did not move. 'Not just yet,' she said. 'Not before I've told you what, deny it as you will, you are dying to know, ahead of all the people who will hear the story it will make tomorrow, and every scandalous line of it engineered by me!'

Cleo caught her breath. '*Scandal?* What do you mean?'

Rosel nodded her satisfaction. 'Ah, you are hooked. I thought you would be. Too bad, also, that having hinted as much as I have, I shouldn't tell you the rest. It's no secret, after all. Quite the contrary. It's not meant to be. So listen——'

Cleo said slowly, 'You're telling me you're involving Luc in some scandal——?'

'—Of seducing a married woman in his villa somewhere around midnight tonight. Even, perhaps, of having forced her, which would read so much the better; or the worse for tycoon Vidame's reputation.'

'But—you?' Cleo faltered. 'You aren't a married woman!'

'Care to see my ring? Or my marriage certificate? Or even my husband, who will be around on cue, I hope? Perhaps you'd like him to call on you in the small hours, after our coup?' Rosel offered.

'Then you aren't Mademoiselle Rostand? That isn't your name?'

'Strabon, my married one. But as our friend would have recognised that, to his shame, I've had to do my act as Rosel Rostand, to which I was born.'

'You are saying then that Luc didn't know you until you met him through me, but that he knows —or has known—your husband?'

'And his family, including Bernard's young sister, Annick, whom Luc Vidame seduced.'

'*Seduced?* Wh—when?' faltered Cleo.

'Oh, not lately. Five or six years ago. Bernard has had to wait a long time, but he is going to avenge her now.'

'But what do you mean—Luc Vidame seduced her? How do you know?'

'He enticed her to leave home and got her to Paris. She was pretty and young—barely eighteen —what other purpose could he have had than to enjoy her for as long as he fancied her?'

(This wasn't true! It couldn't be—of Luc. And yet——?) Cleo asked, 'What proof have you that the girl went away with him or to him? Did she write to her people or go back to them after she left home?'

'Bernard says she wrote once or twice, but his parents had cut her off and destroyed her letters without opening them. The Strabons are an old Corsican family; the disgrace was more than their pride could take and Bernard, as the only son, had to swear to avenge Annick's honour some day.'

For Cleo, suddenly, it was as if the jagged pieces of a torn picture had been rejoined to make sense of a scene. She was remembering how Rachel Navarre, a Corsican herself, had defended her people's long memories of offence to their family honour. The vendetta no longer demanded blood for blood, but insult had to be made to pay its toll. The *attacar*, the deliberate slight of a woman in public, Rachel had said, was an instance of such an extorted price. And this plot against Luc, Cleo realised with horror, was another. Luc had enticed a young girl from home; in consequence he and she were judged without trial or mercy, and years later the verdict was to be carried out.

Years? *Five* years? Five years ago, someone had been welcomed to Paris on the telephone, someone with a name now—Annick Strabon?

For all her dismay Cleo scorned, 'So your in-laws valued their pride higher than their daughter's welfare? When she wrote Luc might have left her; she might have been ill or without money, and wanted to come home!'

Rosel shrugged. 'We Corsicans don't forgive. But don't blame me—I wasn't there. I hadn't met Bernard then.'

'But you are prepared to ruin a man's reputation over something that happened years ago?'

Rosel shrugged again. 'Bernard is my husband, and if he has a score to settle, he knows he can count on my help.'

'*Has* counted on it and got it, evidently,' said Cleo bitterly. 'As you say, you've "worked" to some purpose on your victim. But how do you intend that the scandal you'll create for him is to get out?'

'And who wanted no part of it—didn't want to know?' Rosel taunted. 'I knew as soon as I whetted your appetite, you'd be as avid for the details as everyone else will be! Well, here's the plan in advance. I'm given time to compromise Luc—about an hour or less should be enough. Then Bernard turns up, with a friend for witness, catches us in mid-operation and tells Luc exactly what the consequences to him and his precious exclusive estate are going to be.'

'Threatens him, you mean?' Cleo asked faintly.

'With all the adverse publicity for the place

which Bernard can spread, and with the success Luc has had, there'll be plenty of envious people ready to listen and to spread it further. Think of the headlines—"Director's Love Nest". Or "La Réserve. Cover For Wide-Scale Debauchery"—' Rosel gloated.

'Shut up!' snapped Cleo. 'You can't do this to Luc Vidame. And one reason why you can't is because you've been fool enough to tell me it's a plot.'

'But too late for you to be able to do anything about it. You can't warn Luc—you haven't a telephone, and I'm on my way, and Bernard and his friend are at their stations.' Rosel stood up and went towards Cleo's shower room. 'You don't mind, do you, if I check on whether I need any running repairs?' she asked with consummate insolence, and as she bent to the mirror, went on, 'And so—little sister-in-law to be avenged, and innocent wife to be saved from ravishment by outraged husband. Nice planning, don't you think? Congratulate us!'

Cleo, who had followed to stand behind her, met the bright malice of her eyes in the mirror and upon a surge of anger, acted.

She stepped back from the threshold of the tiny room in a flash and had turned the key in its lock. Then she dashed for the outer door, opened and banged it shut behind her, and ran.

Down the path from her chalet, down the main

avenue, across to L'Allée Napoléon, along it the hundred metres or so to Luc's villa. His car stood outside, so he was there. But of course Rosel would have made sure he would be. From running and from sick apprehension Cleo's heart was thumping high in her throat as she knocked on the door and waited.

Luc opened to her, stared, and she thought he made a movement to close the door upon her.

But she clung to the jamb, gulping for breath. 'No, Luc, please! I must see you,' she begged.

He said nothing, opened the door wide enough for her to sidle past him, and closed it behind her.

CHAPTER SEVEN

HE wore a short towelling robe over slacks. His hair was rumpled; the head cushion of the divan was dented; a book, face downward, and a wine-glass were on a stool beside the divan. As Rosel had forecast, he evidently wasn't expecting callers.

Hands deep in the pockets of the robe, he stood uncompromisingly before Cleo, waiting. In her panic she longed to shout at him, 'Care! *Care*, can't you, that I'm doing this for you?' But of course he didn't know, and now she was here, the whole thing looked too fantastic, too far-fetched to be told. When she saw he wasn't going to ask her to sit down, she found a chair for herself and sat, fingers locking nervously in her lap. He sat too then, on the divan. 'In no hurry?' he asked. 'Whatever catastrophe you've come to report, it can wait?'

She shook her head, bewildered by the double question. 'Yes—that is, no. It *is* urgent. It can't wait.' She stopped, then blurted, 'You hadn't invited Rosel Rostand to come here tonight?'

Luc frowned. 'At this hour?' He plucked at the opening of his robe to show that his torso was bare. 'Does it look as if I planned entertaining her —not to mention you? Why do you ask?' he said.

'But she has been here? At other times? With you, alone?'

'For a drink before dinner, yes. Why?'

'Not at night? As late as this?'

'Never at night.' Luc stirred impatiently. 'Look, what *is* this spy-mission about Rosel Rostand? What's the urgency of it that causes you to ferret it out at this time of night?'

'Because,' said Cleo with slow deliberation, 'her name isn't Rosel Rostand. It's Rosel Strabon. She's married to a man named Bernard Strabon, who has a younger sister named Annick.'

Watching Luc, seeing from his hardened expression that the information had struck home, she could almost pity him. He muttered, to himself, not to her, 'Annick—Annick Strabon. Yes.'

'You know her? Remember her? Know her still?' Cleo pressed.

'I haven't seen her for some years.'

'But you did, once, persuade her to leave home?'

'Connived at her leaving, helped when she had done it.' Luc added quickly, 'How have you learned about this?'

'From Rosel herself. She came to my chalet a little while ago, saying she wanted to put in time before coming here to see you.'

'As if we had an assignation?'

'No. She said you hadn't, but that when she came she would see to it that you invited her in. Because she had an assignation of sorts—with her husband, to compromise you by his finding the two of you together and creating an enormous scandal against you and the estate.' Cleo spread her hands emptily. 'I know it sounds unbelievable, but that's the shape of their plot against you, Rosel said.'

'So—— But if it's true, why should she have confided it to you?'

'She'd been drinking,' said Cleo flatly.

'And——?'

'That could have made her careless enough to boast about it, or she could have told herself that, with the—the thing being within half an hour or so of being a *fait accompli*, there was nothing I could do about it, and that when the scandal broke, it would be only my word that it was a plot, against hers and her husband's and his witness.'

'A disinterested witness, eh? They seem to have thought of everything!'

'Yes. A man Bernard Strabon was bringing with him.' Cleo said wretchedly, 'I'm sorry, Luc, if you've believed in Rosel; if you've fallen in love with her. Have you?'

His short laugh was scornful. 'About as deeply as I'm ever likely to fall for her type.'

'But you've encouraged her, taken her out, and wherever you've been, she's never been far away!' Cleo protested.

'I thought I could afford to let her have her fun as a predator, with no shame to lose in trying to get her man. I confess I was curious about her determined pursuit of me, but my reasoning stopped short of anything like this,' Luc said.

Only too ready to forgive him for *not* loving Rosel, Cleo said, 'You couldn't have guessed, without knowing her real name.' She paused before adding, 'It—it's the Corsican thing, isn't it? Their revenge against you because of—Annick?'

How she longed to hear him disclaim Annick as he had disclaimed Rosel! But he merely nodded, 'A vendetta in defence of their family honour, yes. But what do you know about that?'

'Rosel said that was what it was, and you and Rachel Navarre once talked about it when I was there.' She waited in hope, but his next remark was practical.

'And so—when may I expect the arrival of the innocent victim of my evil designs?' he asked lightly.

Cleo said, 'Rosel? She won't be coming. She—can't.'

'Can't? Why not?'

'Because I've locked her in my shower room, and there's no way she can get out.' Cleo met his incredulous, quizzical stare for a long moment, then looked away. 'The two men will come, of course,' she said. 'Quite soon now, I should think. But when they do come, you'll be alone.'

Luc's brows crooked upward. 'Alone? Shall I? And where will you be?'

She hadn't faced that one. 'I—I—I must leave before they come. Don't you see, they could make almost as much of finding me or—or any girl here with you as they could of finding Rosel?'

'Of finding you—could they? All the same, you are staying.' As he spoke he rose, went to the door and did something with the lock.

She sprang forward in panic. 'I *must* go! You aren't locking me in, are you?' she pleaded.

He turned. 'On the contrary, I've freed the night-latch, so that our friends won't have to resort to breaking and entering, in order to catch their hot seduction scene. They can walk straight in on it as it's happening—and a pity to cheat them of it, don't you think?'

They had met now, and Cleo shrank from the purpose she read in his eyes. He meant to force her, to play-act the love he could never have felt for her, make use of her being there, for the sake of his whim to turn the tables on the enemies he had made for himself long ago. Dear God, she thought, he could be as cruel and scheming as they!

She backed away from him, hands outspread

to fend him off. 'No, Luc—let me go!' she begged.

He came on, took her by the elbows. 'And where do you propose to go? Back, to mount guard over your prisoner?'

'No. But anywhere. I could make up some excuse to go down to Anne's——'

'At this hour? No. You're staying here until at some time later which suits me, I'll take you back myself to free the lady. In the meantime——'

He was thrusting her backward. For a moment she resisted, balancing unsteadily on her heels, then had to give way. His hands were on her shoulders now, his body the force which pressed her on to the divan, where he straightened and looked down at her before sitting beside her, supporting himself and imprisoning her with one arm arched across her body. His legs were crossed, one foot idly swinging, his pose full of easeful assurance that he had the mastery of her now.

Despairingly Cleo pushed back the hair from her temples. 'Luc, you can't want this . . . want me. You said you didn't!' she pleaded. 'It would be all so false, so—so *animal*, when we——'

'—Are so out of practice that we can't go through the motions for a deserving cause? Speak for yourself,' he advised insolently. 'I think I'm equal to the occasion, and you've only to feign enthusiasm as, in their own interests, women always can.'

She shuddered with distaste, but his hands were now at her back, lifting and crushing her to him as his body stretched alongside hers in the close intimacy which had always been the prelude to the heady ecstasy of their lovemaking. How could he dissemble so?

His fingers were at the back zip of her dress; it dropped clear of her shoulders. He had already shrugged out of his robe and now they were flesh to flesh, warm and clinging, as his mouth sought hers in hot demand of its response. There was nowhere for her arms to go but around him, and she clung in a drowning hold—a drowning of all resistance to his possession of her, a drowning which paradoxically brought her to life in his arms, drawn towards the sun of the desire he could arouse in her, every straining nerve urging her to give and to take, to possess and be possessed.

If there had been thought she would have hated what he was doing, hated herself for yielding to a need of him which transcended all prudence, all self-pride. But where thought should have been there was only a primitive sensuality a-quiver with delight as his searching hands travelled over her, touching, caressing, discovering, and his lips plundered her softness as if they found treasure there.

She felt an inner turning to him, a willingness prepared to deny him nothing, however deeply false his purpose. The dream had to come to an end, but—Not yet, not yet!—she was praying as passion surged towards climax . . . in the same moment as the dream splintered and broke to the rude awareness that sweet privacy was no longer theirs. She and Luc were not alone. They had an audience of two who stood and watched, and shame returned, and anger at Luc's stagecraft, and the sick memory of her surrender. They all flooded in upon her in a cruel tide.

Luc turned and stood, reached for his robe. He addressed the intruders coolly, 'Well, gentlemen, have you seen what you came to see—and use? Or could it be that you are disappointed?'

The two men seemed nonplussed. They stared in silence. Then one of them, swarthily handsome in a scarlet shirt, demanded, 'Where is Rosel? What have you done with her?'

'Done with her?' Luc affected pained surprise. 'With Madame Strabon, *alias* Mademoiselle Rostand? Why, nothing! Were you expecting to find her here?'

The other man scowled. Through gritted teeth he said, 'She has been here—at your invitation, Vidame. So where is she now?'

Luc looked blankly about the room. 'Not here, as you see, gentlemen. Not surprising, that, as, lacking any invitation from me, she would hardly be so bold as to visit me at this hour—would she?' he insinuated, adding, 'I'm right in recognising Bernard Strabon, am I not? Brother to little Annick Strabon and now the husband of the absent Rosel?'

'You know very well who I am,' growled Strabon. 'And if you are trying to deny you planned to seduce Rosel tonight, as you once seduced Annick, then you'd better think again. Denial is just not good enough.'

Luc said, pseudo-plaintively, 'I *am* thinking again, and do you know, I'm quite sure I had no designs on your wife's virtue tonight! Nor, believe me, at any other time. I've even found it quite easy to resist *her* designs on my own! What's more, had she been so rash as to invite herself tonight, she would have been particularly unwelcome at the *rather* private session I've been enjoying—with my wife.'

Cleo gasped with shock and Bernard Strabon took a literal step backward. 'Your *wife?*' he echoed. 'You haven't ever married—Rosel said so!'

'Foolish Rosel—who doesn't know everything, and isn't as clever as she meant to be. For I'm right, aren't I, in supposing that my alleged seduction of her was planned; that your catching us in mid-adultery, so to speak, was also planned, and all of it for the purpose of blackening me and my affairs in as much publicity as you could achieve?' Luc suggested. 'I *am* right—yes?'

'And we'll do it still,' Strabon muttered. 'And you know why, Vidame!'

Luc agreed, 'Oh, I know why—to avenge Annick. But will you, can you make scandal out of an incident which didn't happen and for which my wife can give me a complete alibi? If I were you, I shouldn't try, my friend. You can only fail. So if I were you again, I'd collect Rosel from wherever she's hiding and get off my estate—all three of you. Hold your tongues and I won't sue you for trespass and attempted blackmail. But get out by dawn at latest—*and that's an order*!' From sarcastic banter Luc's tone had turned savage, and Bernard Strabon did not attempt to question his dismissal.

He said sullenly, 'I don't know where Rosel is, if she's not here.'

'But I do,' said Luc.

'Where, then?'

'Ignominiously locked in a shower-room. You came by car? You did? Then follow us in mine —Cleo, darling?' He held out a hand to her. She took it and followed him blindly. Play-acting to the last, she thought, and was still thinking it when a furious Rosel had been released into the care of her husband and he, she and their dumb witness had driven away.

As the hum of the car faded Luc drew a long

breath. 'I need a drink,' he said. 'Have you anything in the cupboard?'

Cleo gave him the cognac she had denied to Rosel. 'For you too?' he invited as he poured.

She shook her head wretchedly. 'Do you realise you told those people I was your wife?' she questioned.

'Of course. It was deliberate, the truth, and necessary. If they had caught me with any other woman than you, they would still have had some case for scandal. As it is, they have none.'

'But——?'

He appeared to read her thought. 'Don't worry,' he said. 'It won't go any further, I'm convinced. To admit to anyone the fiasco of their finding me making love to my wife would put them in an impossible position they won't be likely to invite.'

Cleo said bitterly, '*Pretending* to make love, you mean.'

'Ably abetted by you. I congratulate you.'

Her heart was crying—Didn't he know? Had nothing of her deep-felt need got through to him? A small hope died. Nothing had changed. He didn't mean to acknowledge her as his wife to anyone who mattered. It had been a ruse as calculated as his lovemaking—and as successful, but he didn't mean to make it public. She also sensed that, though he had as good as admitted his responsibility for Annick Strabon, both to her and to Annick's brother, he had no intention of explaining it to her, gaining her sympathy, asking for her forgiveness. As his wife she had the right to know. But pride forbade her to ask. Pride, and the dread of his refusal to tell her.

He finished his drink and set down his glass. 'On the whole, it's been quite a night,' he commented.

'Yes——'

'But still an hour or two of it left for sleep.' He went to her and tilted her chin between finger and thumb. 'You're tired. Go to bed—and thank you,' he said.

Cleo nodded dumbly and watched him go. Her choking appeal, 'Luc, *please*—love me!' beat emptily on the door which had closed behind him.

Rosel's moonlight flitting from her chalet was a nine-days' gossip for the office and the estate. But Luc's reactions to her departure remained unknown and there was no one to suspect Cleo's part in it. Anne, musing philosophically that it was just as well they stipulated payment in advance, crossed Rosel's name from future mailing lists, and a new client was installed in the chalet within a matter of days. Except in poignant consequence for Cleo, Rosel Strabon had left no visible footprints behind.

The holiday season was waning. Now there

were more departures than arrivals, but as Anne's pregnancy progressed, Cleo found herself with more than enough to do. Now she sat in committee with Anne and Richard and Luc, ostensibly as minute-taker to the meeting, but quite often her opinion was asked. If only her relations with Luc had been different, she could have seen a career opening up for her. As it was——

She often wondered how much, if anything, Rachel Navarre knew or had heard from Luc about his affair with Annick Strabon. Piecing together the scraps of knowledge she had— Rachel and Luc had known each other since their teens, had lost touch and renewed it at some unrevealed later date, except that Rachel had then been in law-practice in Paris. So if that time had coincided with Luc's seduction of the girl, had Rachel known of it, known the Strabon family in Calvi, known Annick in person?

If so, Rachel might still have been in Paris when Cleo had overheard Luc welcoming Annick there. For this was how Cleo convinced herself it had been—unless Luc were involved with more than one woman at the time of his marriage, it must have been Annick at the receiving end of that telephone call, and as she always did, Cleo shuddered at the memory of his comments on his marriage and on the ease with which she had fallen to him ... sharing the joke with Annick.

Rachel might know. But of course it was impossible to question her. In her view Cleo could have no reason for curiosity about Luc's past. Anything she had revealed to date had been incidental to something else. Unless Luc chose to tell her himself, Cleo despaired of ever learning the truth about Annick. For when the further thought occurred that if Rachel knew about Annick, she almost certainly knew of Luc's marriage, Cleo abandoned her theories, it being obvious to her that Rachel did not know Luc was married, any more than Anne did, or Richard. Luc had kept his cynical secret well, convincing Cleo that only he could confirm or dispel the image of Annick Strabon on which he had uncaringly allowed her jealousy to feed.

But there she had not reckoned with the twist of chance of which Rachel was to be the agent.

Rachel came often to La Réserve, on business with Luc or with Richard, and on an afternoon when she had an appointment with Luc, she arrived to find Cleo alone in the office.

'Luc had to fly to Ajaccio unexpectedly,' Cleo told her.

'Yes, I know,' Rachel nodded. 'He phoned me. But I can get all the papers I need from his villa. I've a key here.' Making no secret of her having the freedom of entry to Luc's house, Rachel riffled through her bag to produce not only the key but an opened letter. 'I must remember to leave this for Luc,' she said of it. 'It is from Mignonne, a young Corsican friend of ours who is abroad. I had a birthday this week, and she always writes for it, and I always pass on her news to Luc.'

Something clicked in Cleo's brain. 'Mignonne —darling?' she queried the name in English.

'Only a pet name. Her real one—Annick. Annick Strabon. She was a very late baby in her parents' marriage—a long space between her and her older brother, Bernard. She always went as Mignonne at home, and she was probably spoilt as a child. But she survived it to turn into a very personable young woman with a brain she wasn't allowed to use.'

Cleo's thoughts whirled. At last Luc's *mignonne* on the telephone was taking real shape. 'Personable'? Did that mean beautiful? Clever? She echoed faintly, 'Not allowed to use?'

'In that, she was no more frustrated than most Corsican daughters of the good old families who couldn't aspire to careers,' said Rachel. 'Mignonne's much older sister was a nun, and if she wasn't willing to follow Berthe into a convent, she could only stay at home, doing nothing until she married. Which wasn't good enough for our young friend. She rebelled as I, being luckier in my parents, hadn't needed to. I was encouraged to make a career.'

Cleo searched her memory. 'Was she—Mignonne, Annick—the girl you mentioned once as having successfully got away?' she asked.

'Did I? Yes. She longed to earn her own living, and with Luc's help and mine, she escaped the net. Luc encouraged her to get to Paris. He paid her fees at night school, and I took her into my office for practical training as a secretary. She got a job in the Ministry of Foreign Affairs, married an American lawyer and went back with him to New Jersey, where they still are.'

'And her people?' asked Cleo.

'I'm afraid they reacted badly. She wrote home often, until it was clear they didn't mean to reply and she had to accept that they had finished with her.' Rachel flicked the letter on the back of her hand before returning it to her bag.' I suppose, she added, 'there are people who would blame Luc and me for our part in the affair. But Mignonne wasn't one of them, and I've always thought we did right to help her. If we hadn't, she would have been doomed to a soured spinsterhood, for she was so keen to work that she couldn't trouble to attract men. So that if she married at all, it would probably have been in desperation, and not for love as she did, once she had proved herself as more than a mere daughter.'

Because she had to know, Cleo asked, 'Was

Luc in love with her, do you think?'

Rachel exclaimed, '*Mon dieu*, no! She was a plain, earnest little thing, hardly more than a schoolgirl, and at that time Luc could command all the glamour any man could want.'

And only married another plain, earnest little thing when it was to his advantage, thought Cleo bitterly. Aloud she asked, 'How long ago was it that you and Luc took Annick Strabon under your wing?'

'M'm—something over five years ago,' Rachel calculated. 'Luc came here shortly after we had settled her, and she was training with me for a couple of years.' Rachel rose, snapping shut her bag. 'I must get on,' she said, and went, leaving Cleo with a sense of having thrown off a load of her own making which she had carried painfully for too long.

She was Sinbad, and Annick was her old-man-of-the-sea whom she had finally dropped from the back of her suspicions of Luc. She longed to shout the news to the four walls and the roof; to run to Luc, clamouring, 'I've been a jealous fool. Forgive me——' until she chilled again to the memory of how he had joked with Annick about the ease of his capture of herself in the marriage which had been necessary to his ambition.

At the thought Cleo's brief euphoria faded and died. For *that* had been Luc's overt, admitted and unforgivable cruelty—his trapping her into marriage for the money's sake. That wrong was too real and lasting for there to be any abject running to him, pleading mistaken jealousy and begging his forgiveness for her suspicion that he had betrayed her with Annick. Nor could she forget his having allowed Richard and Anne and even Rachel to believe he had conceived and developed La Réserve without capital of his own.

She knew he had the funds he had bought with his marriage to her. Whatever they had amounted to, he must have been able to use them as security for the loans he had negotiated since, and she despised the false pride which had claimed otherwise to his friends.

And yet—oh, to feel his arms about her again, his demanding lips on hers! For that, every nerve within her ached.

CHAPTER EIGHT

THE last big event of La Réserve's summer calendar was its regatta, attracting craft from all round the island and even from some Sardinian harbours. Anne joked of it and her coming confinement that it could be a neck-and-neck race between them. To which Richard threatened, 'You'd better see to it, madam, that the baby doesn't beat the regatta to it. There's too much work involved.' But that, Cleo knew, was Richard concealing his anxiety for her. He was far more nervous of the outcome than was Anne, who carried on in happy confidence, tending her garden, driving the communal car and putting in all the hours at the office which Richard would allow her.

She claimed there was no reason why she should not go on working until the date of her going into hospital, and did so until ten days or so before the regatta, the car, an ageing, hard-worked model of increasingly capricious habit, let her down by refusing to engage its gears on a return journey from Bonifacio, and the consequent struggle to ease it to a garage was a strain which she admitted to Cleo she could have well done without.

That night she was willing to go early to bed with enough of a heightened temperature to alarm Richard. But she was in the office as usual the next morning when Luc arrived to decree that Richard should take her away for a few day's holiday.

Anne protested, 'We can't go now. The regatta——' She appealed to her husband. 'Tell him it's impossible. There's far too much to do.'

Luc interposed, 'Richard has already agreed, I'm afraid. You could go inland to the mountains, or up to Calvi, or across to the mainland if that's your fancy. But you are going, woman, and that's an order.'

'We could go after the regatta; after the baby.'

'Complete with crêche? Then too, if you like. But you are also taking a break now, and Rachel and Cleo and I will cope without either of you.'

'But Cleo has never had to deal with a regatta!'

'Then it will be all experience for her,' Luc retorted unhelpfully. 'It's only paperwork, after all, and I hope you're not suggesting I can't organise a regatta with one hand tied behind my back?'

'Oh, Luc——!' But with both men ranged against her, Anne had to give in. But before she and Richard left she grumbled sympathetically to Cleo, '*Paperwork*, the man says! You'll be lucky if the Bonifacio pastrycooks don't go out on strike, just as you've settled the catering, or you can't get insurance cover against a force ten gale on the day. Paperwork! Rather you than I, my child, without so much as a husband to protect you from the Big Wrath if you fall down on anything Luc asks of you, even the impossible!'

But Luc did not ask for the impossible—merely for a workload which kept Cleo at full stretch all the hours there were.

There were advertising, catering for estimated crowds, spectator tickets to be printed, race-entries to be registered, withdrawals scratched, invitations to honorary judges to be written to Luc's dictation and sheaves of all the other correspondence which the affair demanded. At the same time she had to fit in her routine duties of welcoming and despatching clients, interpreting, smoothing out difficulties, doing Anne's share as well as her own.

But she enjoyed the busyness. While it lasted it kept the problematical future at bay and there was challenge to proving to Luc that she was equal to the task. Now she did not bother to close the office at noon, but brought cheese and fruit from her chalet and ate them while she worked on.

Luc, finding her there, had made no comment on her having given up her lunch-hour, and subsequently when he needed to see her, made that his time for calling in. Sometimes he came on foot from his villa, sometimes by car on his way elsewhere. Three or four mornings after the Marlowes' departure he invited Cleo outside and pointed to the car which had brought him.

It was a-gleam with newness, a smaller model of the powerful make he usually drove. 'Yours?' Cleo questioned. 'You're making a change?'

'No. This is a replacement for the jalopy you three have been sharing until now. That one is past its best, as it demonstrated to Anne the other day. This will be easier for you and her to handle. It's automatically geared,' Luc said.

Cleo approached the car and traced the line of its maroon trim on olive green with a respectful forefinger. 'Not easier for me,' she said. 'I've never driven an automatic.'

'Then it's time you learned. There's nothing to it. A couple of lessons, and you'll agree. When can you take the first?' Luc demanded.

'You mean I must make an appointment with the garage to take one?'

'No, I'll administer it. When are you free?'

'Oh—Well, not today. I've a huge backlog of work to get through.'

'Then we'll make it this evening. Close the office at five, and I'll bring the car round to your chalet at half-past.'

She supposed he meant to drive round the estate, but when she joined him he drove west out of the main gate along the coast road through hamlets above tiny bays and vineyards which stretched inland to the mountains. He demonstrated the theory of the automatic as he drove, and on a level kilometre of road, changed places with her.

She drove gingerly, nervous of his critical eye upon her. But as she got the feel of the car's response she agreed that its control was easier. 'Anne and Richard are going to enjoy driving this,' she said.

'I hope so.' A little further on he stopped her, got out of the car himself and told her to drive on.

'Alone?' she queried doubtfully.

'Yes. As far as you like, and come back for me.' He sat down on a hump of granite by the roadside, and watched her through the drill of moving off.

She drove on through the next hamlet and some distance beyond it to a crossroads where she turned and went back to him. 'You need some practice on our gradients,' he approved. 'But you seem to have the hang of it so far.'

'I think I have,' she said, adding as he rejoined her and took over the driving seat, 'I wonder automatics aren't more favoured than they are —in England, at any rate.'

He said to that, 'Some people prefer the challenge of gear-changing. I do myself. I need to feel

I've the mastery of the thing, not it of me.'

'I can well believe that.' She spoke impetuously, and as quickly regretted making a personal issue of his remark when his swift glance put her on the defensive.

'Meaning——?' he invited.

She felt her colour rise. 'Nothing. Or—well, it's typical of you, isn't it, that you need to manage situations ... people, as you manage cars, and you don't care who or what gets bruised in the process?'

'On the contrary, I've never smashed up a car in my life,' he denied coolly.

She had gone too far and knew it. But his deliberate misunderstanding roused her further. She said, 'It was you who said you needed to manage cars. But *I'm* talking about situations you've managed; people you've—you've trodden on, on your way to where you are. Me, for one. You *used* me. You used our marriage to earn the money which must have got you the estate, and because your pride couldn't bear your friends to know *how* you had bought it, you manipulated them into thinking you had achieved it on flair and foresight, without a *sou* in cash behind you! And then——'

'And then?'

Out of breath and appalled by her own tirade, Cleo had stopped. But in answer to that cold prompting she had to go on.

'Then?' she countered. 'Then the lesser things. Your letting me come here, knowing who I was; making me stay—for Anne's convenience, managing things for her as well as managing me. And making use of me as—as you did and, to my shame, I allowed you to, the night you had to foil Rosel Strabon, to save the estate's reputation, to save your own. Oh yes, Luc Vidame, "managing", making us all dance to your tune, is something you do *very* well, very well indeed!'

There; it was out. All the poison of the canker she had carried around for too long, and though ashamed to hear herself mouthing it, her voice finished on a shrewish note—high, uncontrolled, between mirthless laughter and querulous tears.

Luc's reaction was swift, wordless and shaming. Turning in his seat, he administered a sharp slap to her cheek, turned front again and started the car, ignoring her gasp of outraged surprise.

'How dare you——?' she choked on a breath.

Not looking at her, 'Merely shock-therapy for hysterics,' he said.

'I am *not* hysterical!'

'Then quit using the accents of a fishwife for a distorted version of our circumstances in which you seem to believe. But let me remind you—you married me willingly; you wanted me—then. Later you left me, equally of your own will. In consequence of which, as I see it, you earned no right to judge any subsequent actions of mine in relation to the estate or whatever. You take my point?'

Sobered now, she nodded. 'If I have to,' she allowed reluctantly.

'Good.'

'Even about your disowning me, but still claiming me as your wife to those men when it suited you?' she insinuated quietly.

'On your arrival here——'

'Which you'd purposely arranged!'

'For my own evil ends, as you'd see it, no doubt. Very well—when you came, it suited us both to disown each other. And when I claimed you the other night, very shortly before that I'd gained an impression that you rather wanted to be claimed——'

So she hadn't, as she had hoped, since, hidden from him her longing, her yearning for him to take her in love to the very peak of fulfilled desire. She allowed her long silence to answer him before she said, 'You were only acting a part, and I was trying to act it too.'

'Then you've missed a vocation on the stage,' he retorted, showing her he did not believe her, and that, even if they had not been interrupted, he would have denied her the crowning ecstasy she had craved. He did not speak again, and nor did she. He left her at her chalet, saying of the car, 'Use it when you need to; you are competent enough,' before he drove it away.

But she did not use it. He must have meant it principally for Richard and Anne, and she decided to leave it in the carport as a surprise for their return.

She saw Luc only once again that week. He called in at the office, expecting the regatta programmes to have come from the printers, which they had not.

'When did you send in the copy?' he asked Cleo.

'On Saturday—no, not until Monday. We had to hold over for some late entries which hadn't come in,' she told him.

'Monday? Wasn't that asking too much?'

'I thought so, but Rachel said it always happened; it always had to be a rush job, but that the printers had never let you down yet.'

'Then they'd better not this time.' Luc reached for the telephone. 'I'll have a word with them.'

'They will make delivery this evening without fail,' he told Cleo afterwards. 'Can you be here when they come?'

'I'll wait until they do. Will you want to see the programmes?'

'A sample will do for checking. Send one up by one of the men.'

'To the villa?'

'No, to my apartment. I shan't be there all the evening. I'm taking Rachel out to dinner, but the thing can be left with the concierge. And see that

I get one, whatever time the delivery is made, will you?'

Rachel, thought Cleo after he had gone. It was strange that somehow she couldn't be jealous of Rachel any more. For love of Luc she had to be glad for him that Rachel had endured. For obviously he valued her and respected her, and that hurt Cleo far less than the thought of the cold-blooded affairs he had indulged from time to time, according to Anne.

At Cleo's lowest moments, they rankled. She conjured images of the women who had fallen for him and whom he would have encouraged to the point of his own boredom with them—so far and no farther, Anne had said, until he had discarded them. Cleo didn't blink facts; she lived in no fool's world of belief that during the years of their separation Luc had been as celibate as she had been for preference, but her imagination wanted to forget these passing affairs. If he no longer loved her, she would rather he loved Rachel who had lasted for him as a friend since their youth. She liked Rachel and in any office crisis had come to admire her calm and to depend on her good sense. During these days of working together they had come to the edge of an intimacy which, Cleo felt, would allow her to ask Rachel about her relationship with Luc. For the time was coming when whatever future Luc

planned for his broken marriage had to be faced
—hadn't it?

That night the dusk of a leaden, airless day
was falling before the printers' delivery was
made. Cleo checked the contents of the parcel
and selected a couple of the programmes to send
to Luc.

By one of the estate men, he had said. But
they were all doing overtime, erecting spectator-
stands for the regatta and, tempted by the
thought of the welcome air there might be on
the heights of the Citadel, she decided to do the
errand herself.

She took the road to Bonifacio in the old car
and urged it up the steep cobbled streets to the
old town. As she had expected, the higher the
climb, the cooler the air, but in the narrow alleys
the early gloom had brought on the lights in
most of the houses, and a light was showing in
Luc's apartment. Cleo had expected he would
already have left, but with no cause to see him,
she obeyed his order to leave the small parcel
with his concierge.

The woman accepted it reluctantly. 'Monsieur
is at home. You could deliver it yourself,' she
said.

'It doesn't matter. I was to leave it with you.
If you would see that he gets it tonight——?'
Cleo suggested firmly, and escaped to an under-
tone of grumbles, a veritable cacophony of

thunder overhead and the downpour of rain to
which the heavy clouds had been building all day.
The rain on the long-dry road was causing steam
to rise from the *pavé*, itself swiftly becoming a
slimy glass. She would have to drive carefully
on the downhill run, but she was well used to
the car by now and should be able to hold it on
its brake. She was glad she hadn't brought the
automatic; unfamiliar with it, she mightn't have
known how to control it in a skid.

She did a three-point turn in the narrow street
and switched on her lights; gathered a reasonable
speed in a lurching, bucketing progress caused
by each sudden and necessary use of her brake.
Until—knowing that one of the steepest gradients of the road lay shortly ahead, she began to
use the brake in anticipation of it, pressed down
the pedal with little effect, pressed it further—
no response; clamped it at floor-level and in a
cold uprush of fear, recognised its failure.

The car ran on, making its own speed, increas-
ing it, in spite of her despairing reach for the
handbrake and her frenzied clutch upon the
steering-wheel as if she hoped to hold back the
car's weight by her own puny force.

She could only steer and visualise in horror the
inevitable end when steering would be of little
avail to check the car's wild swerves and glissades
on the greasy roadway. Then the crash must
come. A collision with another vehicle? A somer-

sault? An explosion and a spreading fire? She was thinking in lurid pictures, not in words—of herself, loosening her safely-belt, opening a door and leaping for her life; of a heap of crumpled metal and strewn glass and seeping oil; of a road-bordering wall, broken and gaping, with the car astride the crumbled stonework and she—where?

Time must have passed, but she could not have measured it. For her there was only the springing sweat of fear in palms and on brow, the cruel drop of the road ahead and the hurtling mechanical box which was her prison, before there was the jutting wall at a corner, the steering-wheel slewing from her grasp, the car bouncing and rebounding from the impact, the headlamps shattering—none of which registered with her as pain took over and the merciful darkness of unconsciousness came down.

Someone was bending over her, very close, watching her. Other people, not far off, were whispering—ss—ss—ss—whispering about her. Cleo opened her eyes. How long since she had seen with them? She didn't know. It was daylight. She was in bed in a strange room, and no one was bending over her, and nobody was whispering in a corner. Odd——

She looked about her. The lightness of the room, its minimum of furnishing, its antiseptic smell said 'Hospital' even to someone so hazy of brain that she could imagine seeing and hearing people who weren't there. But why was she in bed in hospital? Because her head ached? Not badly enough, surely? Because—yes, perhaps because of that knotting pain under her ribs. Now she was fully awake; to draw breath hurt, and deep breathing agonised. Panting after the experiment, she lay back on her pillow, recognising that pain, vaguely remembering its beginning. Beginning, but not going on. Nothing going on after that ... Before it, the car, noise, a hurtle of stone—and darkness. And all her fault because she had tried to drive a car without brakes downhill. Or no—that wasn't quite so, was it? She hadn't known, before she started, that the brakes were faulty. But how long ago had it all happened? Last night, probably. But who had found her and brought her here? And what had become of the car? A 'write-off', they would have to say of it, she supposed. And it hadn't been her car to wreck!

The door, held slightly ajar on a pad, was opening. A nursing Sister came in and across to the bed, smiling.

'Awake, Madame Vidame? Back with us again at last? That's good. And how are you feeling?' she said.

Cleo stared. She had thought she was awake, but she couldn't be. Or *they* couldn't be—calling her 'Madame Vidame' as if——! But that was nonsense. This nurse was certainly awake and starchily real, however inexplicable her mistake. Cleo began, 'I'm not——' and stopped, wondering how, between wrecking the car and landing herself in hospital, she had ceased to be Cleo Tyndall and become the Madame Vidame whom no one here knew. That is, no one but herself—and Luc. And as Luc wasn't involved, had she, in some moment of confusion, told them her name was Cleo Vidame? She tried again—'I'm not——', but the nurse took her up quickly. 'You are not very sure what happened to you, or where you are?'

'I'm in hospital, aren't I?'

'Yes. This is the Hospice de la Vierge, and you were brought in after your car accident on the Rue Caporel—you remember that now?'

Cleo nodded. 'I was driving down from the Citadel, and the car-brakes failed—last night.'

'Last night? Today is Wednesday, *chérie*!'

Cleo echoed, 'Wednesday? It can't be! We've *had* Wednesday this week!'

'Of *your* week, perhaps. But this is the next Wednesday. You were brought in on Friday night, and you have been unconscious, except for one or two intervals, ever since.'

'Friday? And this is Wednesday? Then the Regatta—on Sunday?'

'Highly successful, one understands. But your

husband spent very little time at it. Most of the day he was sitting here, at your bedside, madame.'

'My—husband?'

'It was he who found you after your accident. His was the next car to follow you down the Rue Caporel, and he drove straight here with you. But you don't recall any of that?'

'Nothing. Was I out when he found me? And what has been wrong with me since?'

'You had suffered a cruel blow on the head and you have broken several of your ribs—that is the pain you must be feeling now. But it will lessen in time and in so young and healthy a body the ribs will heal. We don't strap them any more; Nature does the work for us. But the concussion—that did worry us when you failed to come round. Every day that has passed Monsieur Vidame has been demanding more specialists for you, from Ajaccio, even from Paris—— But now, madame, would you like to see him?'

Cleo's heart pounded. 'He—Monsieur Vidame is here now? Then may I?' she asked.

'For a very few minutes, while I report to your doctor and our neuro-consultant in charge of your case.' The Sister smoothed the bed, poured fresh lemonade into a tumbler, tweaked at a flower and rustled out.

Cleo lay back, apprehension plucking at her nerves. Why had she asked for Luc to come to her? Why, instead, hadn't she gained time by asking to be allowed to take a bath, to do her hair, to look at herself again in a mirror after these lost five days of oblivion? They would have understood she would want to appear as normal as possible to her husband, and she might have prepared something to say to Luc when he came. As it was, he could come round that door at any minute now; there could be no rehearsing of what he might say, or she reply, but their eyes would meet across the room, and she knew there would be no hiding of the utter bewilderment in her own. He had claimed her to them as his wife. *Why?*

There was a knock. She hadn't expected that, and she answered it with a croak.

Then Luc was there—but not at a distance across the room. In a couple of strides he was by her bed, looking down at her, his dark eyes eloquent of—something, his mobile mouth working.

The question she wanted to ask would not come out. Her eyes brimmed with weak tears. 'Luc,' she whimpered, 'I—I'm sorry. About smashing the car. The brakes failed and I panicked——'

'There was nothing you could have done.' His voice was rough. 'But why were you driving it at all?'

'I was afraid I didn't know enough about the

new one yet. It—it was you who found me?
Was I——? Was everything a frightful mess?'

'You had passed out. Until I found you were
breathing, I thought you were dead. When the
crowd gathered and the ambulance came, they
asked me if I knew you——'

He had given her the lead himself. 'And you
told them my name was—Vidame?'

'That you were my wife. I travelled with you
in the ambulance and gave them all the par-
ticulars they wanted when we arrived.'

'Under your name?'

'Yes.'

'But, Luc—why?'

'Because it gave me the right to claim you. Because I had denied you for far too long, and perhaps until it was too late. Ah, love'—suddenly
he was on his knees to her, reaching for her
hands, bowing over them—'don't you see that,
though you might never know of it, it was the
only thing I could do for you? That, however
little my doing it meant to you, I had to make you
my wife again—if only in name?'

Cleo stared at his bent head. *This* was Luc—
humble, pleading, saying incredible things? Was
she dreaming? Or were the last cruel months of
his rejection of her the bad dream? No, they
were the reality; she had lived through *them*, she
knew. And so had he. He had chosen to reject
her, and yet, if she had heard him aright, he was

begging of her the understanding and forgiveness which he had once dared her to offer him. And for some reason he seemed to think she wouldn't care either way!

If he had not imprisoned both her hands, she would have smoothed the sweep of his dark hair, telling him something with the tenderness of the gesture. She drew a long breath, and as if he sensed her recoil from the pain of it, he looked up.

'Did you think I shouldn't be grateful?' she questioned.

'How could I tell how much it mattered to you? It was something I had to do,' he said.

'Without counting the consequences for yourself? That having—acknowledged me, everyone will have to know? Richard and Anne and——'

'They know already. They came back late on Friday night. I told them the truth that night, and Anne was in Ajaccio hospital to have her baby—a boy—on Saturday.'

'And—Rachel Navarre?'

'Rachel has always known that I was briefly married and that my wife left me. But I had never named you to her, and being Rachel, she had respected my silence.'

'And hearing about me now—she didn't mind?'

'Rachel? Why should she?'

'Because I've had to wonder whether she loves

you, and whether, when you were rid of me, you would marry her. I like Rachel and I wanted you to be happy, but——'

He shook his head at her. 'My heart, you have it all wrong. Rachel is married to her job, and she and I have had for years *une amitié amoureuse*—which is what it says, a loving kind of friendship. But that's not love as I understand it; as I thought you and I understood it once.'

'If you had understood it in the same way as I did, you would never have let me go. You would have explained the truth about Annick Strabon,' she accused him.

'You had judged me on a few overheard words of a telephone conversation! And so—what *was* the truth about Annick?'

'Rachel told me. Without knowing that the name meant anything to me, or that you had left me to believe Rosel Strabon's lies about your having seduced her. You hadn't, Rachel said. You had only schemed with her to get Annick away from home and into the job she wanted.'

'And you were able to believe Rachel?'

'Of course.'

'Yet you didn't let me guess that you knew I hadn't been unfaithful to you with Annick?'

Cleo said nothing for a moment. Then, 'There was—there still is—the other worse thing. You've never yet denied the truth of that gossip-column's scoop—that you'd married me just in time to collect the fortune you were expecting, and that you had picked on me because I was *ingénue* and flattered and biddable and probably too much in love to resent your making use of me so.' She drew another painful breath. 'That has stayed with me, I'm afraid. It's always hurt much more than jealousy of Annick—or of anyone else you may have made love to since,' she finished.

Luc's clasp upon her hands tightened. 'I'm a man, Cleo,' he said. 'I have a man's normal appetites. Do you suppose that, having lost you, I haven't looked for someone to replace you?'

'No, I know you must have done,' she acknowledged.

'And always failed. *Always failed*, do you hear, and usually before I was tempted to betray the memory of you?'

'The memory of me as I was then—in love with you?'

'And as I was—and am—in love with you. The memory of us together, of what we were to each other. You say I picked on you. My darling, I *chose* you because I couldn't help myself. Chose you for your freshness, your difference, your trust in me, the tenderness and the fire I sensed in you for all your innocence——'

'Don't you mean my immaturity? Over the phone that day I left, you were saying I was "easy", that I'd fallen to you like an unripe

apple, that I'd made you a willing gift of myself
—gloating about your success!'

He nodded. 'That was Annick on the line, telling me she would be in Paris with Rachel very
shortly—you know, you say, about that. And
yes—I *was* gloating, letting her congratulate me,
marvelling that any girl as young as you should
have such an instinct for love and being loved.
In that you *were* "easy"—utterly full of promise, and I couldn't believe my luck. As for my
timing, you've got to believe the truth—that if
I had met you long before or years later, if I'd
been free I'd have chosen you just the same.
Chosen *you*. Wanted *you*!'

Cleo longed for him to convince her. He
sounded so desperately sincere. And yet——!
'Are you saying that our meeting and your
marrying me would have happened anyway, at
any time, and not just because your marriage en-
abled you to claim the money?' she queried.

'What else?' he parried.

She withdrew one of her hands from his and
thoughtfully traced the line of his jaw with a
forefinger. 'I'd give anything in the world to believe you,' she sighed. 'If you did love me, it's
possible, I suppose. But there was that lie——'

Luc caught at the finger and put it to his lips.
'Which lie?' he murmured.

'Well, though you must have used the money
to start building La Réserve, Rachel and Richard

and Anne and everyone, I suppose, are convinced you got the banks on to your side by sheer flair and opportunism, and no one could have led them to believe that but you. So what was that but your false pride talking, not wanting to admit you had capital behind you; that you weren't as business-astute as they thought?'

For the first time the lines at his eyes creased with a hint of laughter. 'The Vidame pride talking—how right you are!' he agreed. 'But not lying, my heart. I did manage to convince the banking-gnomes that this coast needed a marina development, and that if I didn't build it, somebody else would. And so that cash is still in a Paris bank, multiplying healthily, and the lot of it in your name, not mine.'

Cleo stared, needing to moisten her lips before she could speak. 'You had it, but you never used it? Oh, Luc——!'

'Scorned to use it, to prove to you that I did marry you for love and not for it. And if I never saw you again, to prove to myself that, since it had come between us, I *could* do without it.' He paused. 'Does that do anything for you?' he added.

'But—when we did meet again, why didn't you tell me, explain?'

'Why didn't you ask me, instead of magnanimously "forgiving" me?'

'You were so cold, so distant, so contemptuous of me, that I was afraid of you. If you had hated me, as I thought you did, you couldn't have rejected me more.'

'When all the while I was hungry for you. There were times when I could barely keep my hands off you. After your pup of a boy-friend had risked both your lives in Sdragonatu, you took a bath in my villa——'

She flushed, remembering. 'And I was hungry for you, the night you pretended to make love to me, when those men——'

His arms went about her body then, gentle with her torn ribs, as if she might break. 'Say that again,' he ordered.

'S—say what?'

'You know what. Unless you say it again, I shall never believe I heard it.'

She said it again. 'I was hungry for you. Wanted you so much. Loved you——'

'Ah, love.' His voice came muffled as he pressed his face to the softness of her breast, words deserting them both as passion spoke, yearning towards a future when it could be fulfilled.

They were there in silent tableau when the nursing Sister returned. 'I was delayed. I have left you with Madame longer than I intended, but now you must go,' she told Luc, who muttered 'Quack, quack,' irreverently to Cleo's shoulder, before he kissed her lightly and rose obediently to his feet.

The nurse went to Cleo's bed, straightened the coverlet and plumped the pillows. 'Madame must rest. You will have tired her out with your pleasure at finding her recovered,' she said.

'Though if all I've done for her this time is to tire her, I've an idea she is going to forgive me,' said Luc as he went out.

Ten days later the two convalescents held joint court in Luc's villa. The new baby was there too, but for him the party's laughter became his lullaby and the champagne flowed unheeded. He puckered his face and clenched his fists and determinedly slept.

Rachel and her father were there, and Richard and Luc, toasting the double *raison d'être* of the party, Cleo and Anne, each of them aglow for her own happy cause of being congratulated. They had not met until Cleo had been discharged from hospital the previous day, and she had been diffident and nervous of the encounter.

But Anne had been splendid. She and Richard must already have expended whatever shock and bewilderment Luc's revelation had caused them, for she had fewer critical questions for Cleo than she had had good wishes. She claimed she had always wished Cleo could be a permanence at La Réserve, and she considered that for her to be remaining as Luc's wife was a real overspill of clever management on the part of fate.

Cleo had murmured gratefully, 'You are good —not even blaming us for deceiving you as we did.' To which Anne had retorted,

'Blame you? My dear girl, all Richard and I feel is that you both deserved to have had your silly heads knocked together for your having wasted so much good marriage. And if there's any more nonsense of that sort between you, I warn you, one of us may do it yet!'

'I don't think there'll be any more trouble of the same sort,' Cleo had smiled.

'There'd better not be,' Anne had threatened dourly.

Cleo had felt that Rachel might be kind, and she was, saying that somehow she had hardly been surprised. No, not her Corsican second sight at work, but in Cleo's and Luc's company she had sensed a tension, an awareness of one for the other which wasn't natural between comparative strangers. And having known of Luc's broken marriage, she had occasionally done some imaginative sums in which two and two had made an absurdly but just possible five ...

'I've told Luc his pride was a fool to let you go as it did. But keep him this time. Don't fail him again,' she begged Cleo, and Cleo promised again, 'Never—like that.'

The talk had ranged; the future, including that

of the baby, had been discussed; glasses had clinked, the champagne bubbled, and the blue-green dusk of a golden autumn day was falling when Richard was the first to set down his empty glass. 'Well——' he said, and Anne took her cue. 'Lovely party,' she told Luc. 'But we must go.' Rachel and Monsieur Navarre stayed a little longer. Then she and Luc exchanged their customary parting kiss, and Luc and Cleo were alone.

He swung her round to face him, but held her at arm's length.

'So?' he said. 'What was it this time—defiance or invitation—which?'

She knew what he meant. Yesterday, when she had been packing in her chalet, before moving to Luc's villa, she had come upon the black and silver dress which she had hidden in the hope of forgetting it. She had unfolded it, smoothed it out, and on a mischievous impulse had worn it tonight. Luc had made no comment when she had appeared in it, and until his question she thought her gesture had gone unnoticed.

Glad that it hadn't, she laughed up at him. 'Perhaps a little of both,' she teased. 'I haven't forgotten that the last time I wore it, you threatened to tear it off me.'

He drew her close. 'And might again, though for a different reason,' he murmured against her hair.

'What reason?'

'You shouldn't need to guess.'

They both laughed and for the moment their love-play of words was enough. But as his restless, searching hands moulded her slenderness to the taut contours of his body, it was a vibrant, shared desire which spoke instead. His lips sought hers demandingly; oblivious of the bruised frame of her ribs, his hold tightened, causing her to gasp.

He drew back, contrite. 'I hurt you, my sweet?'

'A little.'

'Badly?'

'Exquisitely,' she said, and went, sinuous, pliant and willing, into his arms again.

Harlequin

COLLECTION
EDITIONS OF 1978

**50 great stories
of special beauty
and significance**

$1.25
each novel

In 1976 we introduced the first 100 Harlequin Collections—a selection of titles chosen from our best sellers of the past 20 years. This series, a trip down memory lane, proved how great romantic fiction can be timeless and appealing from generation to generation. The theme of love and romance is eternal, and, when placed in the hands of talented, creative, authors whose true gift lies in their ability to write from the heart, the stories reach a special level of brilliance that the passage of time cannot dim. Like a treasured heirloom, an antique of superb craftsmanship, a beautiful gift from someone loved—these stories too, have a special significance that transcends the ordinary. **$1.25 each novel**

Here are your 1978
Harlequin Collection Editions...

Original Harlequin Romance numbers in brackets

ORDER FORM
Harlequin Reader Service

In U.S.A.
MPO Box 707
Niagara Falls, N.Y. 14302

In Canada
649 Ontario St.,
Stratford, Ontario, N5A 6W2

Please send me the following Harlequin Collection novels. I am enclosing my check or money order for $1.25 for each novel ordered, plus 25¢ to cover postage and handling.

☐ 102	☐ 115	☐ 128	☐ 140
☐ 103	☐ 116	☐ 129	☐ 141
☐ 104	☐ 117	☐ 130	☐ 142
☐ 105	☐ 118	☐ 131	☐ 143
☐ 106	☐ 119	☐ 132	☐ 144
☐ 107	☐ 120	☐ 133	☐ 145
☐ 108	☐ 121	☐ 134	☐ 146
☐ 109	☐ 122	☐ 135	☐ 147
☐ 110	☐ 123	☐ 136	☐ 148
☐ 111	☐ 124	☐ 137	☐ 149
☐ 112	☐ 125	☐ 138	☐ 150
☐ 113	☐ 126	☐ 139	☐ 151
☐ 114	☐ 127		

Number of novels checked @
$1.25 each = $ _____

N.Y. and N.J. residents add
appropriate sales tax $ _____

Postage and handling $ ___.25

                            TOTAL $ _____

NAME _____
                    (Please Print)
ADDRESS _____

CITY _____

STATE/PROV. _____

ZIP/POSTAL CODE _____

AB ROM 2251

Offer expires June 30, 1979

What readers say about Harlequin Romances

"Your books are the best I have ever found."
P.B.* Bellevue, Washington

"I enjoy them more and more
with each passing year."
J.L., Spurlockville, West Virginia

"No matter how full and happy life might be,
it is an enchantment to sit
and read your novels."
D.K., Willowdale, Ontario

"I firmly believe that Harlequin Romances
are perfect for anyone who wants to read
a good romance."
C.R., Akron, Ohio

*Names available on request